SKINK NO SURRENDER

ALSO BY CARL HIAASEN

Hoot
A Newbery Honor Book

Flush

Scat

Chomp

SKINK
NO
SURRENDER

CARL HIAASEN

ALFRED A. KNOPF
NEW YORK

THIS IS A BORZOI BOOK PUBLISHED BY ALFRED A. KNOPF

All rights reserved. Published in the United States by Alfred A. Knopf, an imprint of Random House Children's Books, a division of Random House LLC, a Penguin Random House Company, New York.

Knopf, Borzoi Books, and the colophon are registered trademarks of Random House LLC.

Visit us on the Web! randomhouse.com/teens

Educators and librarians, for a variety of teaching tools, visit us at RHTeachersLibrarians.com

Library of Congress Cataloging-in-Publication Data
Hiaasen, Carl.
Skink—no surrender / Carl Hiaasen. — First edition.
p. cm.
Summary: With the help of an eccentric ex-governor, a teenaged boy searches for his missing cousin in the Florida wilds.
ISBN 978-0-375-87051-4 (trade) — ISBN 978-0-375-97051-1 (lib. bdg.) — ISBN 978-0-307-97406-8 (ebook)
[1. Mystery and detective stories. 2. Missing children—Fiction. 3. Wilderness areas—Fiction. 4. Florida—Fiction.] I. Title.
PZ7.H493Sk 2014
[Fic]—dc23
2014006036

The text of this book is set in 12-point Goudy.

Printed in the United States of America
September 2014
10 9 8 7 6 5 4 3 2 1

First Edition

For Doug Peacock,
who keeps the fire burning

ONE

I walked down to the beach and waited for Malley, but she didn't show up.

The moon was full and the ocean breeze felt warm. Two hours I sat there on the sand—no Malley. In the beginning it was just annoying, but after a while I began to worry that something was wrong.

My cousin, in spite of her issues, is a punctual person.

I kept calling her cell phone but it went straight to her voice mail, which was Malley chortling in a British accent: "I'm in the loo. Ring you back later!" I didn't leave a message, and I didn't text, either.

In case somebody else had her phone.

Somebody like her dad, who's my uncle. He takes away Malley's cell like twice a week as punishment for acting up, acting out, whatever. Still, even when she's in trouble at home, she always finds a way to sneak out to the beach.

A few turtle people were scouting the shoreline, waggling their flashlights. I walked north, as Malley and I usually did. We'd never seen a turtle actually laying her eggs, but we'd found several nests. The first thing you notice is the flipper tracks leading up from the water's edge. Logger-heads, hawksbills and green turtles leave trenches like a mini–dune buggy when they drag their heavy shells across the sand.

After the mother turtle finishes depositing her eggs, she covers them with a loose, churned mound. Every time that Malley and I came across one, we'd call the state wildlife office and they would send an officer to mark it.

First, wooden stakes are tapped into the sand to create a rectangular perimeter outside the mound; then hot-pink ribbons are strung from one stake to the next. You can go to jail for messing with a turtle nest, so the officers put up a warning sign. Still, every so often some random idiot gets caught stealing the eggs, which are sold as a romantic ingredient in certain places.

Pathetic but true.

The phone chirped, but it wasn't a text from Malley; it was my mom asking where the heck I was. I texted her that I was still down by the water, and that no savage criminals had tried to snatch me. Afterwards I tried Malley's number once more, but she didn't pick up.

So I walked on alone until I came to a marked nest that I didn't remember seeing the last time Malley and I were there. The dig was new and soft. I picked a spot outside the warning ribbon and sat down holding my base-ball bat, which Mom makes me carry for protection when-ever I go to the beach after dark. It's an Easton aluminum model left over from when I played Little League. I feel dorky carrying it, but Mom won't let me out of the house if I don't. Too many creeps in the world, she says.

The slanted moonlight made the waves look like curls of pink gold. I lay back, folded my arms behind my head and closed my eyes. The wind was easing, and I heard a train blow its horn to the west, on the mainland.

That wasn't all. I heard the sound of breathing, too, and it wasn't my own.

At first I thought: *Turtle*. The breaths were damp and shallow, like air being forced through a broken whistle.

I sat up and looked around: No sign of tracks. Maybe it was an old bobcat, watching me from the dunes. Or a raccoon—they like to dig up loggerhead nests and chow down the eggs. I slapped the Easton in the palm of my left hand, which stung. The noise was sharp enough to scare off most critters, but it didn't frighten whatever was breathing nearby.

Leaving seemed like a smart idea, but I got only fifty yards before I turned and went back. Whatever I'd heard couldn't be very large because otherwise I would have spotted it; there was really no place to hide on an empty beach under a full moon.

Approaching the turtle nest again, I put down the Easton and cupped my ears to muffle the sound of the waves. The mysterious breathing seemed to be coming from inside the rectangle of pink ribbons.

Could it be a crab? I wondered. *A crab with asthma?*

Because new turtle eggs don't make a peep. That I knew for a fact.

Carefully I stepped over the border of ribbons and crouched on top of the nest. In and out went the raspy noise, slow and even. I leaned closer and saw a striped soda straw sticking out of the sand. Through the exposed end I could feel a puff of warm air whenever the underground creature exhaled.

No more than three inches of the straw was exposed, but that was enough to pinch between my fingers. When I pulled it out of the mound, the in-and-out noise stopped.

I stood dead still on my heels, waiting for a reaction. Honestly I wasn't trying to suffocate the critter; I just wanted to make it crawl out so I could see what the heck it was. My thought was to take a picture with my phone and text it to Malley.

The world's sneakiest crab, right?

But then, as I was peering at the spot where the soda straw had been, the turtle nest basically exploded. A full-grown man shot upright in a spray of sand, and my heart must have stopped beating for ten seconds.

Built like a grizzly, he was coughing and swearing and spitting through a long, caked beard. On his chiseled block of a head he wore (I swear) a flowered plastic shower cap. Even weirder, his left eye and right eye were pointed in totally different directions.

I vaulted back over the ribbon and snatched up my baseball bat.

He said, "Get serious, boy."

After catching my breath, I asked, "What are you do-ing here?"

"Gagging, thanks to you."

I tried to apologize but I couldn't put the words to-gether. I was too freaked.

"Let's have your name," the man said.

"R-R-Richard."

"They call you Rick?"

"No."

"Ricky? Richie?"

"Just Richard."

"Outstanding," he said. "I like your parents already."

"Dude, you can't sleep in a turtle nest!"

"What'd you do with my straw?" He brushed himself off. I'm guessing he stood six four, six five. Large, like I said. He wore a moldy old army jacket and camo pants, and he was clutching a dirty duffel bag.

"They'll put you in jail," I said.

"Yeah?" He wheeled in a full circle, kicking violently at the sand with his boots. I covered my eyes.

"See, Richard," he said when he was done, "it's not a real turtle nest."

One by one he yanked up the stakes and tied them together with the pink ribbons. He crammed the whole bundle into his duffel and said, "I was waiting on a man."

"While you're buried on a beach?"

"It's meant to be a surprise. His name is Dodge Olney.

5

Digs up turtle eggs and sells them on the black market for two bucks a pop. One night he's gonna dig up me."

"Then what?" I asked.

"He and I will have a chat."

"Why don't you just call the law?"

"Olney's been arrested three times for robbing logger-head nests," the man explained. "The jailhouse experience has failed to rehabilitate him. I'll be taking a different approach."

There was no anger in his voice, but the slow way he said the words made me seriously glad not to be Mr. Olney.

"Tell me this, Richard. What are you doing out here?"

I don't have much experience with homeless persons, so I was sort of sketched out. But he was an old dude, probably the same age as my grandpa, and I decided there was no way he could catch me if I ran.

Looking up and down the shore, I saw that I was on my own. The nearest flashlight beams were a couple hundred yards away—more turtle people. There was a row of private houses on the other side of the dunes, so I figured I could take off in that direction, if necessary. Pound on somebody's door and yell for help.

"I've gotta get going," I said to the stranger.

"Excellent idea."

"If you see a girl out here about my age? That's my cousin." I wanted him to know, in case he got any crazy ideas. He was aware that in the moonlight I had a good look at his face, those weird eyeballs that didn't match.

"You want me to have her call you?" he asked.

"Don't talk to her, please. She'll get scared."

"Understandably."

"Maybe you should find somewhere else to crash," I said.

He grinned—and I mean these were the whitest, brightest, straightest teeth I ever saw. Not what you expect on a grungy old guy who'd just popped out of a hole.

"Son, I've walked the whole way from Lauderdale on this hunt, sleeping every night on the beach. That's a hundred and thirty–odd miles, and you're the first person to make it an issue."

"It's not an issue," I said. "Just, you know, a suggestion."

"Well, I got one for you: Go home."

"What's your name?" I asked.

"So you can give it to the cops? No thanks."

I promised not to call the police, which was true for the moment. The man wasn't breaking any laws, sleeping underground with a straw for a breathing tube. Really he wasn't bothering a soul, and then I came along and riled him up.

"The name's Clint Tyree," he told me, "although I haven't answered to it in years. Good night, now."

He walked away, along the water's edge. I sat down beside the remains of his fake turtle nest, took out my cell and Googled the name he'd given me, just to make sure he wasn't listed on some child-predator site. He wasn't.

He was, however, famous for something else.

When I caught up to him, half a mile down the beach, I told him that Wikipedia said he was dead.

"Wiki who?" he said.

"It's a community encyclopedia on the Internet."

"You might as well be talking to a Martian." He kept walking, the waves splashing over his boots.

I said, "Dude, I really want to hear your story."

"First tell me about your cousin. You're worried about her."

"Not really."

"That's bull."

"Okay," I said. "Maybe a little worried. She was supposed to meet me here tonight, but she never came, which is weird."

"You tried calling her?"

"Sure. Over and over."

The man nodded. "Hold my eye," he said, and plucked the left one out of his face.

I was home, in bed, when Malley finally texted: "Grounded again. Sorry I couldn't sneak away."

A perfectly believable excuse, except for one hitch. After leaving the beach, I'd jogged the seven blocks to her house and seen that the lights in her bedroom were turned off. Malley was a total night owl; she always stayed up way past midnight. It was only ten-thirty when I'd crouched behind the oak tree in her front yard, watching her window. The room had been completely dark, which meant that Malley wasn't home.

Which meant she couldn't be grounded.

From my bed I texted back: "R u ok?"

"Fine. Call u 2morrow."

Of course I couldn't sleep after that, so I went out to the living room, where Trent was watching television—a cage-fighting match on pay-per-view. I'm serious.

"Your mom's snoring like a buffalo," he said.

"They snore, too? I thought they just snorted."

"Hey, champ, before you sit down? Grab me a cold one from the fridge."

Trent drinks more Mountain Dew than any mortal human on the planet. It's hard to watch, because he slurps the stuff so fast that it drips off his chin like green drool. We're talking *gallons* of sugary caffeine, every day.

I brought him a bottle anyway. Trent is my stepfather, and we're cool. He treats me like a kid brother, and I treat him the same way. He's harmless and good-natured, and dumb as a box of rocks.

"Is that ice cream?" he asked me.

No, Trent, it's a cheese ball with chocolate sauce.

"Want some?" I said.

"Maybe later, champ. You believe these two beasts?" Trent was addicted to cage fights. "Yo, see that? It's real blood," he said.

"Wow." That was the best I could do. The truth is

I'd rather sit through a documentary on Calvin Coolidge than watch two buzz-cut goons beating the crap out of each other in a supersized dog kennel.

Mom married Trent last December, not quite three years after my father had passed way. Dad was an awesome guy, and I miss him worse than anything. He was way smarter than Trent, but he died in a really stupid way. He'd be the first to admit it.

Here's what happened: He drank two beers, hopped on his skateboard and crashed full-speed into the rear of a parked UPS delivery truck. It was a large vehicle, but my father didn't see it in time. That's because he was too busy unwrapping a Butterfingers candy bar while he coasted down A1A.

No helmet, naturally. We're talking about a forty-five-year-old man with a master's degree in engineering from Georgia Tech. Unbelievable.

At the funeral one of his surfer buddies stood up and said, "At least Randy died doing something he truly loved."

What? I thought. *Bleeding from his eardrums?*

Afterwards Mom was a wreck, and she pretty much stayed that way until she met Trent, whose only known hobby is golf. He works as a real-estate agent here in Loggerhead Beach, but business is slow, so he's got an unhealthy amount of spare time. His second-favorite TV program is a cable reality show called *The Bigfoot Diaries*.

To yank Trent's chain, I told him I'd spotted a Skunk Ape on the beach.

"Get out," he said.

"Well, he *smelled* like a Skunk Ape."

"Just wait, champ. Someday they'll catch one of those hairy monsters, and I can't wait to see the look on your face."

Trent is a true believer in Bigfoots, Sasquatches and Skunk Apes, which is what they're called in Florida.

"The one I met had a glass eye," I said matter-of-factly. "I dusted the sand off it for him."

"That's real hilarious, Richard." He tipped the liter of Mountain Dew to his lips and chugged the backwash. "I heard they're gonna start hunting 'em with drones, like they do with the Taliban. How cool is that?"

"Ultracool," I said, and went back to bed.

I fell asleep listening to Willie Nelson, one of Dad's favorites. When I woke up in the morning, there was a text from a girl named Beth, Malley's best friend on the track team.

"She's gone!" Beth said.

"Gone where?" I texted back.

"She won't say! What do we do?"

TWO

My uncle looked surprised to see me. He had on his work clothes. His name's Dan, and he runs a bucket truck for Florida Power & Light.

"Is Malley around?" I asked.

"No, Richard, she left yesterday."

"For where?"

"School. She didn't tell you?"

"I thought her classes didn't start for a couple weeks."

"Come on in," Uncle Dan said. "I just got home from work." Hurricane season he works a night shift because the pay is better, and he's got seniority. "You want some breakfast? Sandy's still asleep."

He poured me a bowl of cornflakes and on top he sliced a banana that was so old and mushy that, honestly, a starving chimpanzee wouldn't have touched it.

"Yeah, Malley flew up for early orientation," he said.

I just nodded while I chewed my cereal, avoiding the funky brown slices.

"She forgot all about it," Uncle Dan said, "until two days ago when her dorm adviser called. But that's Malley."

"Classic," I said.

Uncle Dan and Aunt Sandy were sending Malley to an all-girls boarding school called the Twigg Academy. Basically, they didn't want to deal with her on a daily basis anymore. She's a handful, no question.

Malley had told me the tuition at Twigg is thirty-nine grand a year, not including the meal plan. Add the cost of winter clothes plus airplane tickets back and forth to New Hampshire, and who knows how her parents planned to pay for that kind of an education. Malley suspected they were taking a second mortgage on their house, meaning they must've been semi-desperate.

"It's weird she didn't tell you she was leaving," Uncle Dan remarked, "so you guys could say goodbye."

"No big deal," I said, a total lie.

Malley and I were born only nine days apart. Except for vacations, both of us have spent our whole lives in Loggerhead. I couldn't picture her at a boarding school in a place so cold that car engines froze. Truthfully, I couldn't picture her at a boarding school, period. Malley wearing a uniform to class? No way.

"Did she talk much to you about this move to Twigg?" Uncle Dan asked. "Because we got the impression she was sort of looking forward to it. I think all of us need a break."

"She seemed okay with it," I told him, which was true.

Malley had been incredibly calm and low-key when she told me the news. Where, if it had been me who was getting shipped to some snotty private academy, I would've been highly pissed off.

New Hampshire? Seriously?

Still, I wasn't ready to swallow Malley's "early orientation" story.

To Uncle Dan I said: "She borrowed a book from me. You mind if I go get it?"

"'Course not, Richard." He was attempting to make waffles with a digital waffle-maker that my mother had bought him for his birthday. Programming the thing was complicated enough to keep him distracted while I snooped through Malley's room.

Her One Direction poster was still on the wall. So were Bruno Mars and the Jimi Hendrix Experience— Malley was into all kinds of music. The closet wasn't as empty as I thought it would be, and right away I noticed that she hadn't taken her winter clothes to school. There was a heavy parka that had a hood lined with fake rabbit fur, and a red fleece with the L.L. Bean price tag still attached.

Okay, it was only August. Maybe she planned to come home for a visit and get her coat and fleece before the weather up north got cold, or maybe Sandy was going to pack everything and send it to her.

Or maybe Malley hadn't really flown to New Hampshire.

Her laptop was gone and her desk was cleaned out, except for one drawer. Inside was a white envelope that had the initials T.C. printed on the front, above an address in Orlando.

T.C. was a guy named Talbo Chock, who was older than Malley. He lived near Disney World and supposedly was some hot club DJ. Malley had never met him in person, but she'd made friends with him online, which was beyond stupid. I'd told her so more than once.

Even though the envelope wasn't addressed to me, I opened it.

A note in Malley's handwriting said: "Talbo, pleeze don't forget about me when I'm away at Twitt's 'boring' school. Try to land a gig in Manchester so we can finally get together!"

Included with the note was a wallet-sized photo. It was her class picture from last year, before she got her braces removed—a picture she didn't like, and one she would never have given to a guy she was trying to impress.

Malley always kept some cute selfies on her iPhone. She could easily have texted one to Talbo Chock; she could have texted him the note, too.

But the envelope wasn't really meant for T.C., and Malley hadn't simply forgotten to mail it. She'd left it inside her desk on purpose, for her parents to find. I put it back in the drawer.

As soon as I got home, I Googled that street address in Orlando, which turned out to be a motel near Sea World. I called the place, and—big shock—nobody named Talbo Chock was registered there.

Next I looked up the Twigg Academy and dialed the academic office.

"When does early orientation start for new students?" I asked the lady who answered the phone.

"We don't do early orientation," she said.

I called Beth right away to tell her. She wasn't surprised. Her conversation with Malley that morning had lasted barely two minutes.

"She swore me to secrecy," Beth said, "but she didn't tell me enough to even call it a secret."

"What about Talbo Chock?"

"All she said was, 'Don't worry, girlfriend, he's a man of the world.'"

"So was Jack the Ripper."

"I'm scared, too," Beth admitted.

"Let me see what I can find out."

The stranger who'd buried himself on the beach wasn't just a regular homeless person, if there is such a thing. A long, long time ago he'd been governor of Florida—as in *the* governor.

According to Wikipedia, Clinton Tyree was a college football star before going to Vietnam and winning a bunch of army combat medals. After the war, some friends talked him into running for governor, even though he didn't like politics. He campaigned on a promise to clean up all the corruption in Tallahassee, our state capital, and apparently he tried hard. Frustration set in, then sadness, depression—and even, some said, insanity.

Then, one day halfway through his term of office, Clint Tyree flat-out disappeared from the governor's mansion. Nobody kidnapped the man; he just bolted. The politicians who'd been fighting against him said it proved he was crazy, but his supporters said that maybe it proved just the opposite.

All kinds of wild rumors got started, and some of them turned out to be true. According to one Wikipedia entry, the ex-governor became a wandering hermit of the wilderness, and over the years he'd been a prime suspect in several "acts of eco-terrorism." Interestingly, he'd never been arrested or charged with any serious crimes, and it seemed to me that the targets of his anger were total scumbags anyway.

The Web article included interviews with a few witnesses who'd supposedly encountered Clinton Tyree by chance. They said he'd lost an eye, and was going by the name of "Skink." They had differing opinions about whether or not he was nuts. The most recent entry quoted the governor's closest friend, a retired highway patrol trooper named Jim Tile, who said:

"Clint passed away last year in the Big Cypress Swamp after a coral snake bit him on the nose. I dug the grave myself. Now, please let him rest in peace."

Except the man was still alive.

I found him only a mile or so up the beach from where

he'd been the night before. He'd constructed another fake turtle nest, though he hadn't yet concealed himself beneath the sand. He was kneeling outside the pink ribbons, calmly skinning a rabbit.

"Roadkill," he explained, when he caught me staring.

"There's a deli on the corner of Graham Street. I can get you a sub."

"I'm good, Richard." The shower cap was arranged on his head in the manner of a French beret. In the light of day I could see the color was baby blue.

"You didn't walk very far today," I said.

"Nope."

"How come?"

"Maybe I'm feeling too old and broken down."

He *was* old, but he looked solid and tough as nails, as Trent liked to say about the cage fighters on TV.

"They had your picture on the Internet," I said, "from like forty years ago."

"No doubt I've aged poorly."

"Even without the beard I could totally tell it's you."

It was some beard, too. The night before, in the moonlight, it had looked distinguished, like Dumbledore's. Now I could see how ungroomed and patchy it was. To the twisted tendrils Skink had attached what appeared to be broken seashells—until you got a closer look.

"Are those what I think they are?" I asked.

"Bird beaks."

"Okay, that's not funny."

"From turkey vultures, Richard."

"But . . . why?"

"Kindred spirits," he said.

In the sunlight I saw that his good eye was a deep forest green, and that the artificial one—the one I'd cleaned for him—was brown and shaped differently than the other.

"What's the latest on your cousin?" he asked.

"Not good. I think she's run off with some dude she met online."

"Meaning, on the computer."

"He's older than her," I said.

"How much older?"

"Old enough to drive, obviously."

"That's unsettling." Skink wrapped the rabbit meat in a rag. The fur he carried up to the dunes and tossed into some sea grape trees. Afterwards he asked me what I planned to do about Malley.

"Go tell her parents, I guess. Today I texted her and called a bunch of times, but she's not answering."

"Is that like her?"

"Sometimes," I said.

He sat down a few feet away. I told him how Malley had lied about going to early orientation. "The note she left was totally bogus, to fake out her mom and dad."

"Tell me the name of her new boyfriend, Richard."

"Talbo Chock." I spelled it for him, though it was just a guess on my part.

"I'll make a call," he said.

"Want to borrow my phone?"

Skink smiled. "Thanks, but I've got my own. All incoming calls are blocked except one."

"Hey, why did your friend Mr. Tile tell that reporter you were dead?"

"Because I asked him to. Come back in an hour or so."

While the governor made his private call, I walked to a surf shop on Kirk Street. My father used to hang out there, so the owners know me. Dad bought all his boards there, and so do my brothers. Before going off to college, they used to surf every day. There's no beach in Gainesville, so now they're suffering.

I'm not a surfer, but I like board shorts and flip-flops; that's basically my official summer uniform. I was looking through a rack of new Volcom shirts when my phone made a high moaning noise, which freaks people out until I tell them my ringtone is a humpback whale. I walked outside to answer the call.

"'Sup, Richard?" It was Malley.

"Where *are* you?"

"Don't be all mad or I'm hanging up."

I said I wasn't mad, just bummed.

"Sorry about the beach last night," she said. "I forgot about this orientation thing—I must've blocked it out of my mind. Mom was totally pissed, but she got me on a late flight out of Orlando. It was, like, the last seat on the whole plane."

"What luck," I said drily.

"But still I almost didn't make it because airport security found a bottle of vitaminwater in my backpack. Seriously! One of the TSA guys pulled me out of line and made me dump everything out—"

"Vitaminwater?" I had to laugh. Malley was on a roll.

"What's so funny, Richard? Vitaminwater is the bomb."

"Whatever. Why'd you text me that you were grounded at home?" I tried to keep my voice low because I was standing on the sidewalk in front of the surf shop, customers going in and out the door.

"I couldn't call you at the time," my cousin said, "and I didn't want you to be mad that I left without saying goodbye."

"So now you're really up in New Hampshire?"

"Yeah. And this place? The armpit of all armpits, Richard."

Very calmly I said: "Malley, there's no such thing as early orientation at the Twigg Academy. I called and checked."

"What? You. Did. *Not!*"

"You're so busted," I said. "Tell me where you really are."

And she hung up, not exactly an earth-shattering surprise. Malley is legendary for hanging up on people. Usually she calls back in five minutes, ten max, but this time she didn't.

A text popped up as I was heading to the beach: "If you go to my parents, I'll never speak to you again!"

"Knock it off," I texted back.

"I'll tell your mom what happened in Saint Augustine! Swear to God, Richard."

"You would NEVER."

"Don't push me," my cousin texted back.

Suddenly I felt sick. Not barfy sick, just sick at heart.

The governor was collecting crabs when I returned to the beach. I told him that I'd finally heard from Malley, and that everything was fine.

He said, "No, son, it's not."

Then he told me something that made me feel even sicker.

THREE

Talbo Chock completed almost one full tour with the U.S. Marine Corps in Afghanistan. He'd been born in New Orleans and lived there until he was eleven, when his family moved to Fort Walton Beach, Florida. There, Talbo played first-string guard on his high school basketball team. His dad worked at a boatyard; his mother was a bookkeeper and secretary for an Episcopal church.

Talbo had just turned nineteen when the supply truck he was driving got blown to pieces by a roadside bomb in a place called Salim Aka, which Skink said was in the dangerous province of Kandahar. Two other Marines in the vehicle survived their injuries, but Talbo died three weeks later at a military hospital in Germany.

And now somebody had stolen his name, somebody who'd tricked my cousin Malley into running away with him.

"How'd you find out all this?" I asked Skink.

"Reliable source," he said. "The Pensacola paper ran a short story about Corporal Chock's death. It would have been a bigger story—*should* have been—except a hurricane was clipping the Panhandle the same day. The corporal's first name was Earl and his middle name was Talbo, which is the one he went by."

Which explained why nothing popped up when I'd Googled "Talbo Chock," right after Malley befriended him online.

Now my brain was tumbling. "The guy who stole that soldier's name," I said, "he could be a total lowlife!"

"Odds are he is."

"But Malley doesn't know. Malley is—"

"In a bad situation," said Skink. "Now go tell her folks, Richard."

They say everybody keeps at least one secret, and maybe that's true. Mine was an ugly one. I didn't rob a bank or anything like that, but what I did was serious enough to crush my mother if she ever found out. And there was at least a fifty-fifty chance that Malley would narc on me, just like she'd threatened to do. She has a ferocious temper.

So, a selfish part of me didn't want to tell her parents that she'd run off with the Talbo Chock impostor, because I was afraid for myself, afraid of what my mother would do if Malley revealed what had happened in Saint Augustine.

I felt a hard stare from Skink's good eye, the one that actually moved. He said, "What're you waiting for, son?"

"You ever done something you were really ashamed of?"

"Oh, never once."

"I'm serious."

He chuckled. "I could write a whole encyclopedia of mistakes. Hell, I could write an opera."

"About a year ago I did something wrong—something against the law—and Malley saw the whole thing. She's gonna rat me out if I let her mom and dad know she's not really up at boarding school."

"Would you prefer they hear it from the cops," Skink said, "after they find her body?"

"God, don't say that!"

He put down the sack of crabs. "Listen up, Richard." It was the deepest voice I've ever heard, like the rumble of faraway thunder. "Whatever you did that you think is so terrible? It's nothing—I mean, *nada*—when weighed against the life of your cousin."

"Yeah, I know. You're right."

He put a hand on each of my shoulders, not a hard squeeze, but I could feel the strength. "Go," he said.

And I did.

Trent was playing golf, and Mom wasn't home from work yet. Our front door sticks in the humidity, so sometimes you have to give it a shoulder. I grabbed a cold Gatorade from the refrigerator and went to my room and pounded on the mattress with the baseball bat. What was my cousin thinking when she said yes to this jerk? Had she lost her mind?

I got a chance to ask her, because at that moment she called.

"His name isn't really Talbo Chock!" I blurted.

"Duh."

"Then who is he?"

"You didn't tell anybody, right?" she said.

"Where *are* you?"

"Oh, Richard. You think I'm stupid or something?"

I was so happy to hear her voice that I couldn't stay angry. She sounded as chill as always.

"He could be a stone psycho," I whispered.

"Ha! So could I."

"This isn't a joke. You don't know a thing about him."

"You don't know *what* I know," said Malley.

I told her that threatening me about Saint Augustine didn't matter. Even if I stayed quiet, her parents would eventually learn that she wasn't at boarding school.

"All I need is a week," she said. "Then you can tell 'em everything."

"What happens in a week? Why are you doing this?"

Gaily she said, "YOLO," an annoying abbreviation for *You only live once*.

"That's weak, Mal. Only yo-yos say YOLO."

"Gotta go, dude."

After she hung up I checked the caller ID, which said "Blocked." I tried back on Malley's regular number but her phone went straight to voice mail. There was no point leaving a message—the Talbo Chock impostor was probably screening her calls.

When I heard my mother come in the front door, I took a deep breath, counted to twenty and walked out of the bedroom. She gave me a hug and said there were groceries in the car.

I pulled out a chair from the kitchen table. "Mom, sit down."

She looked at me over the top of her sunglasses. "Right this minute, Richard? First let's get the bags from the backseat, before Trent's ice cream melts."

"No, we need to talk now."

"What is it? Something happen?"

"I'm pretty sure Malley ran away."

"Oh." Mom didn't shrug, but she wasn't exactly blown away by the news. "I'm sorry to hear that," she said.

"It's not like the other times."

"How do you mean, Richard?"

"She's not alone," I said. "There's a guy she met online. I think we should call Uncle Dan and Sandy."

Mom took off her glasses. Her face darkened with worry.

"How old is this person?" she asked.

"Malley won't tell me anything. She's being a major b-word." I related everything I knew so far, including the content of the bogus letter she'd left in her desk.

"Has he harmed her?"

"I don't think so, Mom."

"Okay. That's good."

I went to the car and grabbed the grocery bags. Trent's precious dessert, a half-gallon of Heath Bar Crunch, made it safely into the freezer. My mother was already on the phone to Uncle Dan. She was in total courtroom mode, her voice steady and calm.

Mom's a lawyer with a small firm that specializes in environmental cases, going after companies that dump waste into public waters. There's not much money in it, but she gets really stoked about her work. I hear her ragging Trent about all the fertilizer pollution caused by golf courses—the club he belongs to is on the bank of the river, and it's totally old-school. The chemicals that are spread on the fairways leach out if there's a heavy rain.

When my mother gets focused on a situation, things move along briskly. After speaking with my uncle, she made several other calls while I put away the rest of the groceries.

"All right," she said when she was finished. "Now we wait for the police to do their jobs."

"Think they'll find her?"

"I do, Richard. Definitely."

Once Malley learned that the cops were out looking for her, she'd go ballistic. I considered telling my mother about Saint Augustine, just to get it over with and beat Malley to the punch.

I didn't say a word, though. No guts.

"If she calls again," Mom was saying, "keep her on the

line as long as you can. Try to remember everything she says. Any small remark could be an important clue."

"How's Uncle Dan and Aunt Sandy?"

"Scared. Upset. Like any parents would be." She got up and started rearranging the cereal boxes in the pantry. "That cousin of yours, I swear. She has no idea what she's gotten herself into."

"I told her the same thing."

"And what did she say?"

"She just laughed, Mom."

The best thing, of course, would have been for Malley to come back on her own. Part of me almost believed that was what would happen, that she'd just stroll through the front door tomorrow, chill as ever, announcing her adventure was over. Uncle Dan and Sandy would be so out-of-their-minds happy to see her that they probably wouldn't even ground her.

The worst thing would be if she decided she wanted to come home but the fake Talbo Chock wouldn't let her. Even though the police go full-tilt on a missing person case when it's a kid, none of us who were close to Malley could be very helpful. We didn't know the true name of the guy she was traveling with. Didn't know how old he was, what he looked like, where he was taking her.

When the officers came to interview me, and I knew they would, all I'd be able to tell them about the fake Talbo Chock is what Malley had told me.

He's sweet, Richard.

He's funny.

He's like a poet.

I didn't want to think too much about what he really was, the awful possibilities.

After dark I ran back to the beach carrying a flashlight instead of my baseball bat. Near the edge of the dunes I found a small, cold campfire; among the coals were a few animal bones.

Up and down the beach I checked a bunch of turtle nests, but none had a soda straw sticking out of the sand.

The weird old governor was gone.

FOUR

The police launched an all-out search for Malley, and for the next several days my hopes jumped every time the phone rang. There were clues to follow, but no red-hot trail.

On the night she'd pretended to fly to New Hampshire, surveillance cameras at the Orlando airport showed her stepping out of her mom's car at the curb on the departure level. She was wearing black jeans, flip-flops and a gray hoodie. She had a red travel bag on rollers and her backpack. After waving goodbye to Sandy, she entered the terminal building.

Eleven minutes later, a camera on the arrivals ramp— one level down—caught Malley hurrying through the exit doors and sliding into a white two-door Toyota. The driver was a man, though he didn't make a move to help my cousin with her luggage; he just popped the trunk and sat there. It was hard to see what he looked like because he wore a Rays baseball cap pulled snug to his brow, a cheap blond wig and Oakley-style shades. The video was grainy, and the lighting at the airport curb was poor.

Luckily, another camera at the expressway entrance got a photo of the Toyota driving away. Crime technicians enlarged the image to read the license plate, which was from Texas. Unfortunately, the plate had been stolen from an Avis rental car in the airport drop-off lot.

Not a good sign. My mother looked grim when she told me that part. Uncle Dan and Aunt Sandy were frantic. Nobody wants their daughter driving around with some loser who'd rip off a license tag. That meant the Toyota was likely stolen, too.

In other words, my cousin was traveling with a criminal.

I got to see one of the video clips from the airport when a detective came to our house. He wanted to know if I recognized the man driving the Toyota, and truthfully I said no. With his Mariah Carey wig and sunglasses, the guy behind the wheel was totally disguised. All you could make out was a regular-looking nose and thin lips. His jaw was set and he wore no expression whatsoever.

Malley was another story. On the video, she was grinning.

They put out a highway Amber Alert featuring her lame school photo, which I knew would make her furious. The TV stations in Orlando, Daytona Beach and even Tampa broadcast the story, showing a factory picture of a Toyota similar to the one Malley's online boyfriend was driving. They also gave out the number on the

Texas license plate, but Mom said the guy had probably already switched it. Swiped a different tag from somebody else's car, my mother said, or maybe even swiped another car.

Using the pings from cell phone towers, the police were able to trace Malley's phone from downtown Orlando (from where she'd texted me on the night she was supposed to be at the beach) all the way to Clearwater (from where she'd called me and Beth the next day).

After that, Malley's phone had either been turned off or broken, leaving the police no way to track her movements.

The detective who came to speak with me was named Trujillo. He was short and muscular, with a thick black mustache. I'd seen him around town before, and it turned out he was a surfer and knew my brothers.

"Why did Malley run away?" he asked.

"I don't know. Maybe she had an argument with her mom and dad."

"Mr. and Mrs. Spence said no. They said everything was good. She was okay with boarding school was their impression."

"Then it was him," I said. "The fake Talbo Chock. He must've talked her into it."

Trujillo had a small notebook flipped open in one hand. "Did Malley have any boyfriends here in town?"

"No. She thought all the guys at school were dorks

and posers." I told the detective what little Malley had said about her dashing Talbo.

"But she never mentioned how old he was? What he looked like?"

"Nope." I regretted that I hadn't asked her more than once.

"Richard, would you say your cousin was a stable person?"

"She's not wacko crazy, but she's definitely a rebel."

Trujillo said he'd already interviewed Beth and she knew even less than I did. He said Malley had warned Beth to keep quiet about her running away or else she'd tell Beth's boyfriend that Beth liked somebody else, which I knew happened to be true. Beth liked me.

"Richard, did Malley threaten to get you in trouble in some way if you told her parents what really happened?"

"No, sir," I lied.

"If she calls again, I'd like you to keep a log—time, date, exactly what she says. Everything you can think of, even if it doesn't seem important. I'll give you a notebook like mine. The texts you can save on your phone, all right?"

"Sure." I'd already deleted the ones from Malley about Saint Augustine.

Trujillo handed me a notebook and a blue Bic pen. I asked how they were going to find the true identity of the guy pretending to be Talbo Chock. The detective speculated that the "perpetrator" was from the Fort Walton

Beach area and that he must have seen the newspaper and TV reports about the real Talbo Chock's death. Otherwise where would he have come up with the name? Trujillo thought it was even possible that the man might have some personal connection to the young Marine.

"State investigators are up in the Panhandle now," he said, "interviewing Corporal Chock's friends and family members."

"What if Malley doesn't call me?" I asked. "Or call anybody?"

"Well . . ." Trujillo was pondering how to phrase it. "That could mean something bad has happened," he said, "or it could mean she just doesn't want to be found yet."

I'd been carrying my cell 24/7, even when I went into the bathroom. There hadn't been a peep from Malley since she'd called from that blocked number and ordered me to wait a week before telling her family the whole story. By now she definitely knew that I hadn't waited even one whole day; it was all over Facebook, Twitter, YouTube and, of course, the television stations. I'd figured she would phone just to yell at me, or at least call my mother to drop the Saint Augustine bomb.

The dead silence wasn't like Malley. Not her style.

Aunt Sandy and Uncle Dan were constantly checking in, asking if I'd heard anything from her. I felt really bad for them. Sometimes Sandy would be crying, which would make me choke up, too.

After that first week had passed, I wondered if Malley had gotten where she was planning to go. I hoped she had. I hoped she was the one in control.

The Amber Alert remained in place, but the story started fading from the news. A little boy in Wellington had gone missing, snatched from kindergarten by his stepfather. The missing boy was sick and needed special medicine, so his case was now getting all the media attention.

Meanwhile, Mom and Uncle Dan offered a $10,000 reward and chipped in for six highway billboards that displayed Malley's photograph and an 800 number for tips. In the blown-up version of my cousin's class picture, her hair was red (although in person you would call it cinnamon) and the light freckles on her nose looked as bright as a rash. She wasn't wearing her regular smile because of her braces, which she complained had made her look like a constipated squirrel.

Still, anybody who spotted Malley Spence could have recognized her from the billboard.

Several calls came in from people who thought they'd seen her, but the sightings were scattered from one end of Florida to the other. Investigators chased down every lead that wasn't too flaky but came up empty-handed. One caller claimed to have witnessed my cousin arguing with a husky tattooed man at a certain movie theater in Sarasota. He said Malley was struggling with the man and trying to pull free.

Slight problem: The movie house had been torn

down six months ago to make way for a Target. The cops threw the scumbag in jail after he admitted making up the whole story just to get a cut of the reward money. Pathetic but true.

The waiting made me feel helpless and hollow. Sometimes I'd dial Malley's number hoping she'd turned on her cell, but it never rang once. Straight to voice mail, Malley in that weak British accent. For all we knew, her phone could be at the bottom of a canal.

I was spending a lot of time on the Internet—too much time, honestly. I'd bookmarked the website of every major newspaper in Florida, and each morning I'd scroll through a bunch of them checking out the crime stories.

My stomach would pitch upside down every time I saw this headline:

UNIDENTIFIED BODY FOUND

So far there had been three different bodies, but all of them were middle-aged men. One guy got hit by a train on the FEC tracks in Jacksonville. Another they found floating in Lake Okeechobee—probably a drowned fisherman who'd left his ID in his truck. The third was just an old pile of bones that a hunting dog dug up in the Everglades. Mom said Miami drug dealers used to bury lots of bodies out there.

"Don't keep reading that stuff," she said. "You'll get nightmares."

"I don't know why she hasn't called."

"Your cousin loves the drama, Richard. Always has."

"True."

"I'll bet she shows up any day now with either a tan or a tattoo."

"No doubt about it," said Trent.

He was on the couch, eating a pasta salad. All the commotion about Malley's disappearance had sort of put him on the sidelines, since he was somewhat new to the family. Trent actually likes the sidelines, especially during a crisis. He's comfortable not being in a position to make decisions, and Mom seems fine with that.

"My sister Kay ran away once," Trent remarked, "to San Diego."

My mother sighed. "Malley's fourteen. Kay was what—twenty? Which means it wasn't technically running away. Plus she ended up marrying the guy, right?"

"Still, we were worried sick."

"Trent, it's not the same," Mom said. "Not even close."

I closed my laptop and went to my room. Detective Trujillo had given me his business card, so I called him to ask if the police had turned up any new clues. A few false alarms, he said, but nothing solid. The interviews in Fort Walton Beach hadn't led anywhere. None of Talbo Chock's friends or family members could imagine why a stranger would be using his name. His parents were pretty upset about it, Trujillo said.

Lots of people were checking out the Facebook page that Uncle Dan and Sandy had set up, but so far the tips were totally random, dead-enders, just like the phone calls coming in about the billboards.

"Don't give up hope, Richard," the detective said. "This case is still priority one for us."

"Did they find the car, at least?"

"Nine white Camrys have been stolen this month in the state of Florida, none of them in the Orlando area. But we're checking out every case."

"So, basically, we don't know anything more than we did in the beginning."

"In a way, no news is good news," said Trujillo. "Most runaway cases, the kids come home once the excitement wears off."

"What if she *can't* come home? What if he won't let her?"

"You said Malley was aware 'Talbo Chock' isn't this character's real name, right?"

"That's what she told me," I said.

"So it's possible she knows him better than we think she does. Maybe that's why she's not afraid."

It was definitely something to hope for.

"Maybe this whole thing was *her* idea," Trujillo said, "not his."

"The fake name? Or the running away?"

"Maybe both. If only we had her computer, we could find out who she'd been emailing and trace his screen name."

Unfortunately, Malley had taken her laptop with her.

Ever since she'd gone missing, I checked my own emails about a dozen times a day. Her not texting or calling—that I could understand, if she didn't want the cell phone tracked. Yet she could have safely emailed me (or, even better, her parents) from anywhere on the planet.

So why hadn't she? It wasn't something I chose to think about very long.

"Hang tough," said Detective Trujillo. "Call me anytime."

When I came out of my room, Mom waved me into the kitchen, where she was sitting with Trent. She told me she was going to Gainesville for a few days to see Kyle and Robbie, my brothers. They were both doing summer terms at the university so they could take off during winter semester, when the surfing was best. Kyle was majoring in business and Robbie was in advertising.

"I haven't seen the boys since May," my mother said.

She'd been looking forward to the visit for a while, and I didn't expect her to cancel on account of the Malley situation. There was nothing more to be done; the rest was up to the police. Or up to Malley.

"You want to come along?" Mom asked. "A road trip, just you and me."

Normally I would have said yes. I worry about her when she makes long drives alone, and besides, she's fun to travel with. Every fifty miles we switch out our iPods on the sound system; that way, each of us gets to hear the music we like. Plus it's the only time she lets me order drive-through for lunch, when we're on the highway and she's in a hurry. At home it's nothing but healthy food, organic *everything*, except for Trent's Mountain Dews and ice cream.

This time, though, I couldn't go with her to Gainesville. My gut would have been churning the whole trip. What if Malley called needing something, and I was the only one she trusted to help her?

"I think I'll stay home, just in case," I told my mother. "That okay?"

"Of course. Trent will be here."

He looked up and grinned. "We'll have some bro time, you and me."

"Sorry, Mom."

"I understand completely, Richard. There's nothing to be sorry about."

"Idea number one," Trent burbled. "Tomorrow a.m. we go out to the club and hit a bucket or two of balls. Then we grab lunch on the veranda and watch all the old geezers triple-bogey the eighteenth!"

The sad part: That was Trent's idea of a rockin' good time.

Mom had bought me a set of second-hand clubs because she'd wanted me and Trent to bond, but golf is an impossible sport, and I didn't enjoy much about it except watching the gators cruise the lakes. One day I counted five.

For a while I went along with the great golfing project,

and give my stepfather credit—he was incredibly patient. The man really tried. But I was hopeless with a seven-iron in my hands. A menace, if you want the truth.

I'd been hoping Trent would give up on me, but it hadn't happened yet.

"Or we could do some fishing," I suggested, watching Trent's expression go blank.

He wasn't a good fisherman—restless, noisy, uncoordinated. I knew he'd rather be strapped in a dentist's chair than stuck on a boat, trying to pinch a shrimp on a hook.

When my father died, I'd inherited his fourteen-foot skiff. It was in almost-new condition because Dad hardly ever used it. Now a week didn't go by when I wasn't out on the river, sometimes with Malley or my friends but more often alone. Dad's boat had a heavy fiberglass hull and a small motor—a twenty-horse outboard—so I never went too fast or too far. Usually I brought home a couple of sea trout or a redfish, which Mom would grill for dinner. Trent loved to eat seafood but he had no interest in the pursuit.

"Cool. Whatever," he said, for my mother's benefit. "Richard and me'll find something to keep us out of trouble."

Mom went to pack and I took a walk, mainly for a distraction. My cell phone, which for days had felt like a brick in my pocket, started making whale noises when I was halfway to the marina. I nearly tore a hole in my pants trying to get it out.

The call was coming from a blocked number.

"Yo, Richard."

"Yo, Mal."

"'Sup?"

The hand that was holding the phone was actually shaking. Pitiful.

My other hand was fumbling in another pocket for the notebook and pen that Detective Trujillo had given me.

"You okay?" I asked.

"Way better than okay. I am a totally happy camper." She laughed, but it sounded a little tight. I assumed that the bogus Talbo Chock was sitting beside her, listening to every word.

I said, "Where are you? You know I've got to ask."

"And you know I've got to say none a yore bidness, mister."

"Why aren't you calling from your own phone?"

"Battery died, Richard. Don't be so paranoid."

In the background I heard a male voice say something about a drawbridge. A horn sounded twice—some type of boat. I also picked out the cries of terns and gulls. Sea birds, but that didn't automatically mean Malley was near the ocean. Gulls are like flying garbage rats. They love dumps and landfills.

"Just so you don't think I'm a coldhearted bee-atch," my cousin said, "I spoke to Mom and Dad and let 'em know I was okay."

"When? You serious?"

"A few minutes ago, right before I called you. They've

been spazzing, which I totally understand. But I only did what I had to do, Richard. I couldn't make official contact till T.C. and I got to our destination."

"And you're there now."

"We are most definitely here. Oh my God, it's like a postcard."

"Is that good?"

"Gee, I don't know. Is paradise good? It's freaking gorgeous, dude."

Malley didn't sound even slightly mad at me. I should have been relieved, but instead I was worried. She acted like she didn't know the police were searching for her. Was it possible she hadn't heard about the Amber Alert? Only if she and her mystery friend had traveled to someplace remote, where her face wasn't on highway billboards or the TV news.

"What did your parents say?" I was trying to keep her talking.

"What do you think they said? 'Come home, sweetie. We miss you so much.' I only stayed on the line for a minute. Mom started bawling. Dad just kept asking where I was, over and over."

"Do you have money?" I asked.

"Oh, quit worrying."

I had the notebook flipped open, and I was trying to jot down everything she said. The phone was pinned between my ear and my shoulder.

"Malley, this is a really big deal."

"The Twigg Academy was *not* happening. You know me better than that."

"At least tell me how old he is."

"What difference does it make if he's sixteen or sixty?" she said. "You should be happy for me."

"I'm happy as long as you're safe. When are you coming home?"

"Hey, I'm moving forward, okay? I'm not thinking about home, school, past lives, whatever."

I couldn't write half as fast as my cousin was talking.

"Malley, where'd he get the name 'Talbo Chock'?"

"That's personal."

I didn't press her on it, because Detective Trujillo had told me not to say anything that might upset her and cause her to hang up. The longer she stayed on the call, he said, the more information I could get.

"You still in Florida?" I asked.

Malley started to respond, but the male voice in the car said something sharp that I couldn't make out. She told him to lighten up.

"Hey, yo, Richard?" she said.

"I'm here."

"Thanks for not telling anybody when you found out I was gone. You're the coolest of the cool."

My mouth went dry as sawdust. Saying nothing was the same as a lie, and I couldn't force it.

"Mal, I *did* tell someone. My mom. And she told your mom and dad."

Another stiff laugh. "I already know, dummy. That was just a test. You're welcome, by the way."

"For what?"

"For me not blabbing to *su madre* about your little one-man crime spree in Saint Augustine."

"Thanks. Does that mean you aren't mad?"

"No, girlfriend, I'm on island time. Nobody 'round here gets mad about anything."

"Cool. What island?"

"Hey, stop it!" she snapped at the other person in the car. "Don't *ever* do that again."

"Stop what?" I asked. "Malley, you all right?"

No reply.

"Malley?"

"It's all good. Gotta go."

"Wait," I said.

But the line was dead.

FIVE

Right away I called Detective Trujillo to share my notes. Malley's mention of a drawbridge was important, he said, although Florida has lots of drawbridges leading to lots of islands.

"Did she sound okay?"

"At first."

"Then what? She seem frightened?"

I almost answered yes, because I was afraid that the police might ease off the search if they thought Malley wasn't in serious danger, if they decided she was just another mixed-up runaway. But the truth was that my cousin *hadn't* sounded frightened on the phone. Annoyed about something, for sure, at the end of the call. Maybe a little edgy.

"She told whoever she's with to stop something. After that she hung up. Or maybe *they* hung up."

"No 'Goodbye, Richard'?" Trujillo asked.

"'Gotta go' is all she said. Like she was ticked off."

"But not scared."

"I can't say." It was possible that the fake Talbo Chock

had pinched or even hit Malley for saying too much to me. It was also possible that he'd just swiped some of her French fries or changed the radio station in the car, and that's why she'd told him to stop and not ever do that again. Malley ruled over the radio, and she didn't like anyone messing with her music.

"You'll hear from her again," the detective predicted. "Meanwhile, I'll call her parents and tell them she contacted you, too."

When I got home, Mom was waiting beside the car in our driveway. She said she'd only be gone a couple days. I told her to tell the surfer boys in Gainesville I said hey.

"Please let Trent know if you take the boat out," she said.

"He turns off his phone on the golf course."

"He won't be playing golf, Richard; he'll be working. He's got a couple of showings."

"No kidding? That's awesome." I was trying to sound enthusiastic, because Trent hadn't sold a house in eleven months. My mother had been paying all the bills, though she never made a big deal about it.

"Here." She handed me forty bucks. "Just in case."

"No, Mom, I've got some money."

"Now you've got more. I'll call you tonight."

After she drove off I went to the marina and put twenty dollars' worth of gas in the boat and headed out to Cutter Island. I caught a good redfish on a bucktail but I didn't keep it. A school of jacks swarmed in from the inlet, ripping at the finger mullet, and I hooked five or six in a row. They're tough fighters, pure sport. I chased the school around until it got too dark.

After docking the boat, I called Trent, who was watching a show he'd recorded on TiVo—a mixed martial arts match featuring his favorite fighter, Lucifer Rex. The man's real name was Maurice DePew, a factoid I'd dug up on Wikipedia and immediately laid on Trent, just to see his reaction. He'd refused to believe it, of course.

"I'll be home in half an hour," I said.

"Mind getting your own dinner? I just ate and I'm kinda into this match."

Which he was watching for, like, the fourth time. A dedicated blob.

"No problem," I said.

"Tomorrow night we'll go grab some burgers."

"For sure."

I wasn't waiting for tomorrow. On the way home from the marina I hit the McDonald's and ordered a Quarter Pounder, which Mom calls a "cholesterol bomb." I went easy on the fries, but still she wouldn't have approved.

My conversation with Malley spooled over and over, especially the words she'd spoken to the person beside her: *Hey, stop it! Don't ever do that again.*

It wasn't unreasonable to assume that the person Malley had been speaking to was her traveling companion, the bogus Talbo. Whatever he'd done at that moment while she was on the phone, she hadn't wanted to share the details with me.

So deal with it, Richard, I told myself. *Just be glad she called.*

Not wanting to go home and veg out with Trent, I hung around Mickey D's for another hour. Talk about pathetic—who spends sixty brainless minutes in a fast-food joint? I knew Trent was so engrossed in the cage-fight replay that he wouldn't notice I was late. He probably wouldn't notice if the kitchen caught fire.

I kept the cell phone faceup on the table in case my cousin called again. Mom texted to say that she'd gotten to Gainesville okay and was taking my brothers to dinner at some new Thai joint. I was in the middle of texting back, telling her about my fishing trip, when three Loggerhead police cars went flying past. They were heading toward the north beach. A minute later came an ambulance with its siren full blast.

Yet it wasn't until I saw the searchlight from the sheriff's helicopter that I pocketed my phone and ran to see what was happening.

It seems like destiny, how some people turn out the way they do.

Certain kids at school, you just know they're going to become surgeons or engineers or Internet zillionaires.

Other kids are more likely to end up selling cars or hospital supplies or real estate (hopefully with more success than my stepfather).

But a couple of my classmates, they're definitely heading full speed for Loserville. That's a harsh fact in every school in every town. Not everyone wants to work hard, and not everyone has a wonderful life ahead. Certain kids are going to flame out in the grownup world—either crash and burn or flop the old-fashioned, lazy way. Sad but true.

A guy who graduated with my brother Kyle is doing eighteen months in state prison for breaking into a computer store and stealing a laser printer and a boxful of Homer Simpson zip drives. Mom knows his parents and says they're solid people, so what happened? A perfectly sensible question. (My own past isn't exactly spotless, but nothing my mother ever said or did can be blamed for Saint Augustine. That was all me.)

Another dude who used to surf with my brother Robbie got busted for selling pain pills to an undercover policeman. The guy's father is a minister and his mom teaches violin. Maybe they messed up when they were raising the kid, or maybe he was just determined to go down the wrong road, no matter what. It happens.

I have no idea whether Dodge Olney had a rough childhood or came from a good, caring family and just turned out to be a thieving moron. But, seriously, what person with a brain larger than a marble would steal turtle eggs for a living?

Truly a primitive life form, this guy.

When I got to the beach, paramedics were strapping him onto a stretcher. His limp right wrist was attached to the rail by a plastic handcuff—basically, a zip tie. His other arm was in a soft cast. He was unconscious and heavily bandaged. I knew it had to be Olney when I saw the pillowcase full of small leathery orbs, which were being counted gingerly by a stone-faced officer from the wildlife commission.

"Ninety-seven," he said to no one in particular when he was done.

I stepped closer and asked what was going to happen to the eggs. The officer said they would be reburied in a safe place on another beach.

"So, they're gonna hatch okay?" I said.

"Sometimes they do. Sometimes they don't. We'll see."

A crowd had gathered, mostly locals. Mixed in were a few crispy sunburned tourists. A policeman was interviewing a woman jogger who'd witnessed what had happened, so I sidled closer to eavesdrop. She gestured toward the motionless Olney and said she'd seen him digging up a turtle nest. Suddenly, she said, a big bearded man had burst howling out of the sand, and the egg thief began slashing at him with a stake he yanked from the nest site.

"Describe the person who came out of the ground," the officer said.

"Tall and freaky-looking." The woman spread her arms. "This wide."

"Anything else?"

"He had things hanging off his face. Like bones or something."

"Did he say anything?"

"No, but he was singing."

"While the poacher attacked him?"

" 'You can't always get what you want,' " the jogger said. "Those were the words he was singing. He grabbed the stake from the egg robber and threw it up in the dunes."

"Then he struck the poacher with his fist?"

"Yes, sir," the woman said. "Hard."

"How many times?"

"I didn't count. He was wearing, like, soldier clothes."

"Did you see which way he ran?"

"Oh, he didn't run. He walked." The jogger pointed south. "Thataway."

The scenario was easy to imagine. Dodge Olney had been looting eggs from a real loggerhead nest before creeping down the beach and digging up the decoy nest constructed by former governor Clinton Tyree, now known as Skink.

A greedy, very painful mistake by Mr. Olney.

The ambulance hauled him away at high speed. If Mom had been home, my phone would have been ringing like crazy. Every time she hears a siren, she calls to make sure I'm all right. This started right after Dad's accident.

Overhead, the sheriff's helicopter continued to circle, its spotlight slicing back and forth across the waterfront.

A young policeman carrying a camera walked over to the fake turtle nest and began snapping photographs. I headed south, searching for boot prints in the sand, using the flashlight app on my cell.

The beach was nearly empty because everyone had rushed to the scene of the fight, if you could call it a fight. Trent would have called it a beat-down. Dodge Olney couldn't have been more than thirty-five years old, yet he'd gotten his butt whipped by an old fart twice his age. It didn't bother me at all, to be truthful. Anybody who swipes turtle eggs to make money deserves whatever misery comes his way. I had a feeling Mr. Olney would be avoiding our beach for the rest of his days, even if he gave up poaching and turned his life around.

Skink must have stayed close to the water's edge for the first few hundred yards, because his tracks had washed away completely. Finally I found a set of fresh prints in the dry, softer sand—definitely boots, definitely jumbo-sized— and I followed them up through the dunes, erasing them behind me with a palm frond so that no one else could see which way he went.

The boot prints ended at a boardwalk leading to a small gated neighborhood of large oceanfront homes. There were no lights on inside the houses because the rich people who owned them lived up north and came to Florida only in the winter. It was like a fancy little ghost town, and the empty streets sort of sketched me out.

"Governor!" I called out. "It's me—Richard!"

Nothing. No sounds except for the breeze rustling the sea grapes.

"Yo!" I shouted. Still no reply.

I heard the whine of the sheriff's helicopter and crouched in a thick hedge while it swooped over, lighting up the streets like a football stadium. As soon as the chopper was gone, I scrambled out of my hiding place and jogged back toward the beach.

How the man caught up with me, I've got no clue. I never heard him coming, didn't even know he was behind me until an ape-sized hand seized the back of my T-shirt and yanked me to a stop. I nearly peed my pants.

"Stay cool, boy," he whispered.

"Okay. Okay." My heart was pounding like a woofer.

"I need a small favor."

"Sure," I rasped. "Anything."

There was only a slice of moon, but it was bright enough for me to see that Skink wasn't wearing his shower cap. His long damp hair was matted. He stood bare-chested in his boots and board shorts. His army jacket and camo trousers must have been stuffed inside his duffel bag.

"I need you to be my dear, devoted grandson for a little while," he said. "In case someone asks."

"No problem."

"A friend's leaving a car for me at the corner of Askew and A1A."

I knew right where that was. We'd have to go back the same way we had come, possibly encountering police officers searching for the person who'd clobbered Dodge Olney.

"You need to lose those gnarly things in your beard," I suggested.

"Yeah." He unfastened each of the buzzard beaks carefully, as if they were delicate Christmas ornaments.

"Here's our story," he said. "You and I went for an evening stroll on the beach together, okay? We didn't see anything unusual or suspicious. If they ask for my ID, you tell 'em the family doesn't let me carry one because I'm always losing it, I'm so old and forgetful. Tell 'em some days I don't even remember to take a shower."

"But we still love you, Grandpa," I said.

He broke out laughing, a thunderous rumble. As we made our way north, he snatched up a length of driftwood and said, "My trusty cane!" He started faking a limp as we drew closer to the yellowy lights of the beachfront district. I took his duffel, which was heavy. If we were questioned, I'd say that my crazy grandpa took off his clothes and went for a night swim in the surf, sharks and all.

Luckily, nobody stopped us. A single police cruiser remained at the scene of the egg robber's misadventure. The officer at the wheel was writing his report and never glanced up as we passed on the other side of the street.

The car left by Skink's friend was a midsize gray Chevrolet Malibu that needed a good coat of wax. It was the most ordinary-looking car imaginable, which I suppose was the whole point. We found it parked in the lot of a bikini shop, where my brother Kyle had tried repeatedly (and unsuccessfully) to get a summer sales job.

Skink sat down on the driver's side of the Chevy and groped under the floor mat until he found the ignition key. I opened a rear door and heaved his bag onto the seat.

"You're a good citizen, Richard."

"Hey, you're hurt!" I said.

The car's interior lights had illuminated a comma-shaped gash on one side of his head. Although the wound wasn't long, it looked deep.

"See, Mr. Olney didn't want to have an adult conversation. He wanted to be a tough guy." The governor shrugged. "There's a first-aid kit in the trunk. Needles, sutures, iodine, plenty of aspirin."

"Sutures?"

Skink smiled. "Mr. Tile is a thorough fellow."

A whale song rose from my pants pocket. It was Mom calling from Gainesville. I let the phone go to voice mail.

Skink nodded approvingly after starting the Malibu. The gas gauge said full and the engine idled smoothly. With his good eye he studied himself in the rearview mirror, arranging his tangled silver mane to conceal the scalp gouge. Now I could see that it wasn't normal surfer shorts he was wearing but funky old boxers.

"Don't worry," he said to me. "I plan to do some personal grooming down the road."

"Have you got somewhere to hide?"

"Hide?" Another earthquake laugh. "At my age, son, the trick is to keep moving. Always have a new project on the board. That's what keeps you going."

"So, what's your new project?" I asked. "You don't have to tell me if you don't want."

"Of course I'll tell you," the governor said. "I intend to go find your cousin. Want to come?"

SIX

Trent isn't a bad person, not at all. He'd do anything for my mother, and I mean throw himself in front of a speeding train. She says it's better to be with a simple man who really cares about you than to be with some Einstein who treats you like a doormat.

Still, I can't deny that I occasionally take advantage of my stepfather's—how should I say this?—intellectual limitations.

When I rushed in the door after the Dodge Olney incident, Trent was on the edge of the sofa glued to a documentary called *Bigfoot Uncensored*.

"Yo, Richard, sit down and watch this! It's awesome."

"Sorry I'm late."

"Are you late?" He looked at his watch. "Oh, wow."

"The engine on the boat was running rough, so I changed out the plugs."

"Good job. You get somethin' to eat?" Trent had refixed his gaze on the TV screen, where a spacey car salesman from Oregon was telling about the time he picked up a Sasquatch hitchhiking on the interstate.

"That," said my stepfather, "would be *so* radical."

"I would totally stop for a Bigfoot."

"Duh, yeah!"

"I'd take him straight to the Cracker Barrel," I said. "Let him order whatever he wanted off the menu."

"Are you being a smartass again?"

"What's wrong with the Cracker Barrel?"

He said, "Shh. I want to hear this part."

"Hey, Blake and his dad are going camping in Ocala for a couple days. They asked me to come. Mom said it's cool as long as you check it out with Blake's folks."

"*Me* check it out?"

"She's stuck at Home Depot with Kyle and Robbie, picking out new paint for their apartment."

Helpfully I dialed, then handed my cell to Trent. By now I was losing track of all the lies I was telling; the main thing on my mind was finding Malley as fast as possible.

"Hi, this is Richard's stepfather," Trent said into the phone.

The voice on the other end belonged to Beth, Malley's friend. She was pretending to be Blake's mother. Beth has acted in a few plays at the community theater, and she can do all kinds of voices. Impersonating a mom was easy.

I'd prepped her on what to say—how much Blake and his dad were really looking forward to me joining them on their trip.

We're sorry for the short notice, Beth would be saying.

60

"Hey, no problem," said Trent. "This is supernice of you."

Now I had to get out the door quickly, in case Mom called the house. I packed my stuff in, like, three minutes flat. Toothbrush, hat, board shorts, T-shirts, underwear, my laptop and a pocketknife—everything went into my backpack.

Then I grabbed a box of granola bars from the pantry and said goodbye to Trent. He actually pried himself away from the Bigfoot documentary long enough to stand and give me a knuckle-bump.

"Have fun, dude, but be safe."

"Always," I said.

The dull gray Malibu was parked in the driveway of a vacant house at the end of the block, Skink drumming his fingers on the steering wheel. He'd put on his shower cap, which I feared would draw more attention than the gash in his scalp. Also, he was wearing sunglasses with violet mirrored lenses. It looked to me like he'd run a comb through his beard (a good start), but dangling from a cord around his leathery neck was the rattle from a big eastern diamondback.

In other words, the man was not what you'd call inconspicuous.

On the way out of town I recounted my last phone conversation with Malley. "So she's got to be on some island that has a drawbridge," I said.

"Maybe."

"Hey, it's the best clue we've got."

"Tell me about the boat horn you heard on the phone. Maybe a tug? Or a shrimper?"

"I have no idea."

Skink seemed annoyed. "Well, was the pitch high or low?"

"Pretty low."

"Deeper the horn, bigger the boat," he muttered. "Bigger the boat, bigger the bridge."

"Makes sense."

"Check in the glove box, would you? Should be a CD."

Mr. Tile had thought of everything. Skink told me to feed the disk into the slot on the car stereo. A song came on that I recognized. It was called "Run Through the Jungle," kind of a Deep South rocker. My father had known all the words.

"So, this is, like, your personal mix?" I asked the governor.

"Road music, son."

We were heading due west, crossing the state, because the last place Malley had used her cell phone—the city of Clearwater—was on the Gulf coast. Maybe the fake Talbo Chock had friends on an island in that area.

I asked Skink how he'd lost his left eye.

"Long time ago, some dirtbag kicked me in the face."

"No way. Why?"

"They beat up homeless people for fun, he and his buddy."

Honestly, I didn't know what to say.

"But that was the last time they did it," the governor added.

"How come? They go to jail?"

"Ancient history."

The next song on Skink's mix was called "Heartbreaker," by Led Zeppelin, another band my dad liked. I had my laptop open, doing a little research.

"Is this right? You were born in—"

"I'm seventy-one."

"No, seventy-two," I said. "You had a birthday two weeks ago."

"Hmm. Guess I missed the party."

I asked if he'd really been bitten on the nose by a coral snake, like Jim Tile had told that reporter.

"It was a toe, not the nose. My friend was being a comedian."

"Then why aren't you dead from the poison?"

"For three long days I wished I was. Jim kept me up and walkin' so my heart wouldn't stop."

I pointed to the rattlesnake rattle on his neck cord. "What's the story there?"

"He got hit by a tomato truck on Highway 41. I honor his memory."

The governor was a steady driver, a pleasant surprise.

I'd assumed it would be hard to steer a car in a straight line if you only had one eye. A few hours out of town, in the middle of nowhere, he slowed down, swung open his door and snatched a dead crow off the road. Next was an opossum (also deceased), which he grabbed by its hairless pink tail and lobbed into the backseat next to his duffel and the bird.

"I'm starving," he said. "You?"

I shook my head no, politely.

"What story'd you cook up to tell your mom?"

"Nothing yet," I said. "Just texted her to say good night. She's visiting my brothers at college."

"What about Troy?"

"His name's Trent."

"She's gonna strangle him," Skink said.

"No, I'll tell her it wasn't his fault. It was all me."

"Okay, your turn."

"What?" I said. The Malibu was slowing down again.

"See that armadillo up there in the headlights?"

"Yeah, what's left of him."

"Waste not, want not."

"Seriously?"

"Perfect angle for a right-hander," said the governor. "Just lean out the door and grab the flippin' thing. And don't unhook your seat belt!"

"Fine."

As we rolled by, I reached for the unfortunate creature—and whiffed.

The car couldn't have been going ten miles per hour, max. Skink chuckled, put it in reverse and collected the rest of his dinner. Twenty minutes later he turned off onto a dirt cattle road. I helped him build a small fire, but I wouldn't eat any of his roadkill stew. Truthfully, though, it smelled all right. He said freshness was key, and also the condition of the corpses.

"Obviously, flattened is no good," he said.

"Unless you're in the mood for pancakes."

"Show some respect, son."

"Are we camping out here?"

"No, tonight we drive. If you're tired, sleep in the vehicle."

That was all right with me. Every mile we traveled was one mile closer to Malley.

She had run away five other times. Once it happened after she got mad at Uncle Dan for confiscating her laptop, but the other four times she'd bolted simply out of boredom. And when I say ran away, my cousin literally *ran*. Her specialty is cross-country, and good luck trying to keep up with that girl.

Two nights was the longest she'd ever stayed away, and no boyfriends had been involved—only Malley running solo. After each incident Sandy would take her to counseling, and naturally Malley enjoyed making up all kinds of whacked stories to mess with the psychologist.

One time she claimed that in a past life she was Cleopatra, Queen of the Nile. Another time she told the counselor that her parents were so mean, they made her sleep hanging upside down from the ceiling, like a bat.

Her worst-ever excuse: After she came home the last time, Malley told the shrink that she'd run away because Justin Bieber was stalking her. She swore he kept climbing the big oak tree outside her house, waving at her adoringly whenever she peeked out the bedroom window.

The story was especially outrageous since my cousin can't stand Justin Bieber, but here's the amazing part: The counselor actually believed that Malley thought she was being stalked and wrote in his report that she was "clearly delusional." She couldn't wait to tell me.

My cousin is supersmart. She aces any class that she wants to ace, and blows off the ones that don't hold her attention. But even if she were way smarter than the Talbo Chock impostor, it wouldn't help her much if he decided to get rough. Although Malley's almost three inches taller than me (thanks to a major "growth spurt"), she's thin from all the long-distance running. Her arms are like noodles, and I doubted she could punch her way out of a soap bubble.

"Pray it doesn't come to that," said Skink.

I was too wired to nap in the car, so I was telling him more stuff about Malley.

"She ever had any boyfriends?" he asked.

"Not a *boyfriend* boyfriend. The guy she ran away with, she met him in a chat room."

"But you said they met on their computers. This 'chat room'—is it like a library?"

"Chat rooms *are* on the computer," I said. "Come on, dude, they're virtual."

"Stop calling me 'dude' or you'll virtually regret it."

"Why? There's nothing bad about 'dude.' Didn't you see *The Big Lebowski?*"

Skink's good eye turned away from the road and squinted at me. "The big what?"

"It's a movie classic."

"I haven't been to the movies since 1974," he said.

In a way, it was like traveling with a space alien.

A space alien who cussed a lot. I've been leaving out the bad words, even though they didn't bother me at the time. The man went to war for this country and got shot at, so he could talk however he wanted to talk, as far as I was concerned.

Also, he was totally committed to finding my cousin and bringing her home. Maybe his friend Jim Tile had told him about the ten-thousand-dollar reward, but the governor never once mentioned that to me. It seemed unlikely that a person who'd spend his summer chasing turtle-egg robbers was interested in money.

"Are you a fugitive now?" I asked. "Because of what you did to Dodge Olney?"

"Nobody who saw what happened knows who I am."

"Still, the cops will be hunting for whoever did it."

"Not very hard," Skink said, "considering Olney's rap sheet."

He was probably right. Some people would have given him a gold plaque for getting that lowlife off the beaches.

I plugged in my car charger and hooked it to my iPod. "Hey, can we play some of my music?"

"Under no circumstances," said Skink.

A line of trucks was coming the other way, and their headlights were blinding. I shut my eyes and thought about my cousin. Was she in a motel tonight? A tent? Maybe the backseat of that Toyota.

I wondered if she'd brought any money with her, or if the bogus Talbo Chock was paying for all their gas and food. Anybody who swiped license tags would have no qualms about stealing a credit card. Maybe he really was a fabulously talented club DJ, like Malley said, or maybe she'd made up that part, too.

Evidently I fell asleep. Next thing I knew, the sun was up and I was alone in the Malibu, which was parked on the bank of a small brackish bay. What had awakened me was the whale song coming from my phone.

"Hi, Mom," I said.

"Where *are* you?"

"On my way to find Malley."

"Richard, have you lost your freaking mind?"

She'd already spoken to Blake's father, who had been puzzled to hear about the nonexistent camping trip.

"Don't be mad at Trent," I said. "It's a hundred percent my fault."

"You come home right now!"

"I can't, Mom."

"Let the police handle this!"

"No, we've waited long enough."

"Richard, I swear—"

"It's fine, okay? Totally under control."

"But who are you riding with? Who do you even know that's old enough to drive?"

"Mom, it's—"

A hand darted hawk-like through the open window and snatched the phone. Mr. Clinton Tyree was now calmly speaking to my mother.

Unbelievable.

"Ma'am, I want to assure you that Richard is safe and well supervised. He and I have set out to find your niece, God willing. I completely appreciate your concerns—do you have a pen or pencil at hand? I'm going to give you a phone number. The gentleman on the other end will tell you as much about me as he prudently can. He has an outstanding background in law enforcement, so please give him your complete attention. Richard will be in touch with you later. He is a promising young man, as you're surely aware, and he deeply regrets deceiving his stepfather, necessary though it was. Now, here's that phone number. . . ."

That's when I understood how Skink had gotten elected governor. He was smooth as silk when he chose to be. He said goodbye to my mother and handed me the phone.

"Where are we?" I asked.

"The wrong damn place. I'm sorry."

We drove along the waterfront for maybe half a mile. Then he pulled over in the shade of a concrete span, four lanes across. It was tall enough for any tug or deepwater fishing boat to pass under; even a sailboat could make it through.

"That used to be a drawbridge," he said dejectedly. "Long time ago."

The new bridge arched from the mainland to a barrier island where the shoreline bristled with private docks. Once upon a time it was all mangroves. On the Gulf side of the island was a tourist beach. I only knew that because a small plane was flying back and forth, pulling a banner advertising "Happy Hula Hour" at some tiki bar.

"This is where I thought your cousin might be," Skink said. "But last time I was here, there weren't any high-rises. It was a quiet place."

To myself I counted six condo towers, lined up like smokestacks.

"Wonder when they took out the old bridge," Skink said. He was seriously bummed.

"Hey, we'll just keep looking," I told him. "There are plenty of other islands."

"The old snowbirds who own those condos, they don't like waitin' on a drawbridge. That's why it got torn down. Don't want to miss that early-bird special at the Macaroni Grill. Ha!"

He kept on muttering like that until I turned up his driving mix again. Then he settled down. I even made him smile by guessing the title of an incredibly old Bob Dylan number called "Subterranean Homesick Blues." Skink asked how in the flippin' world I knew that one. I explained that my father had loved Dylan and lots of old bands, and that the day after Dad died, I'd downloaded his whole playlist to my iPod.

"Yeah? Then let's hear it," Skink said.

So there we were, rolling along the interstate through downtown Tampa, rocking out to my dad's music. Sometimes when I'd look over at the governor, I couldn't believe he was seventy-two. Other times he looked about a hundred and ten. Now he was like a teenager, shaking a fist and howling the lines in a Pearl Jam song. We had the volume cranked up so loud that I didn't hear my phone ringing.

Later we stopped for lunch at a beachside café in Clearwater, where I got to see Skink eat a meal that didn't have to be skinned or plucked. It was then I noticed the voice messages on my cell. The first was from Beth, asking where I was and if I'd found Malley yet.

The second call was from a blocked number.

"'Sup, Ricardo? Yours truly, checkin' in. Everything here in paradise is just amazingly awesome. Guess what I saw way up in a tree this morning? An ivory-billed wood-pecker! It sounded so lonesome, it made me sad."

On the message, Malley was coughing and her voice sounded rough. When I replayed it for Skink, he raised an eyebrow. "She calls you Ricardo?"

"First time ever. Weird."

"She wants you to pay attention."

"Also, ivory-billed woodpeckers are extinct. I did a project on them for science fair in sixth grade, and Malley helped with the graphics."

"I know where those birds live," Skink said.

"You mean *lived*."

"Only one place in Florida, *Ricardo*, and it's not an island."

"I know that."

"The girl's trying to tell you where she's at."

"And the 'lonesome' part—that means she wants to come home."

"Correct," he said.

"Maybe the fake Talbo won't let her go."

"Assume the worst. That's my motto." With that, the governor got up and strode rapidly toward the car.

I crammed the chili dog into my mouth and hustled after him.

SEVEN

Marine Corporal Talbo Chock could have been buried with full honors at the national cemetery in Arlington, Virginia, but his mother wanted him closer to home. The funeral had been held on a sticky July afternoon in Fort Walton Beach, Florida, a month before my cousin ran away.

During the church service, somebody had crept onto the property and hot-wired a 2007 white Toyota Camry belonging to the pastor. On the front seat of the car was a printout of the pastor's eulogy recalling the short life and brave death of Earl Talbo Chock. The pastor had meant to present the copy of his stirring words to Talbo's parents, but instead it had ended up in the hands of a car thief, who decided to also steal the dead soldier's name.

This fact was relayed to me over the phone by Detective Trujillo.

"Probably not what you want to hear," he said, "but it's progress. The preacher's Toyota has a small hole in the rear windshield that matches one on the car in the security video from the Orlando airport."

"Where exactly on the rear window?" I asked.

"Dead center. Preacher gave his kid a pellet gun for his eighth birthday. Not a genius move."

I didn't tell the detective that I was on the road with a one-eyed former governor, searching for my cousin. We'd already counted twenty-three white Toyota Camrys, none of them carrying a couple that looked like Malley and her Online Talbo.

When I informed Trujillo about my cousin's last phone message, I kept the summary brief. It would have been hard to convince the detective that her mentioning a lost species of woodpecker was a coded cry for help.

Besides, the remote area where Skink and I believed she was being held—*if* she was being held—called for a stealthy approach. A convoy of speeding police cars might spook the bogus Talbo Chock into doing something drastic.

For now, at least, he didn't realize anybody was on his trail.

From Clearwater, Skink took Highway 19, which tracks along the Gulf side of Florida all the way to the town of Perry, where you hang a hard left into the Panhandle. That's the route I'd mapped out on my smartphone. It was the quickest way to get where we needed to be, but very soon we got sidetracked.

A blue SUV blew past doing eighty, the driver tossing an empty Budweiser can out the window. One lousy can, all right?

The governor said the guy was a moron, which he undoubtedly was, and after that I didn't think about it. For sure I didn't look at the speedometer, which would have clued me in that Skink was accelerating to keep pace with the blue SUV. I was preoccupied with my laptop, re-reading a worried email from my mother.

When the SUV slowed down and made the westward turn toward Homosassa, we turned, too.

"Where you going?" I asked Skink.

The look on his face was something different—not angry, or agitated. Just cold as granite. Probably the same expression he wore when he heard the scrape of Dodge Olney's trowel in the sand.

I tried once more. "Governor, what are you gonna do?"

No answer.

"It was just a beer can. Seriously."

He shook his head, like he was disappointed in me.

"Anyway, we don't have time," I said. "We've gotta hurry to catch up with Malley."

"Son, this won't take long."

That was it, as if no explanation was necessary. He just expected me to understand.

The sky was darkening with low storm clouds as the SUV pulled into a restaurant called Bucky's Deluxe Dining. It looked more like a bar. Skink kept going until he found a convenience store. Fifteen minutes later we were back at Bucky's in a driving rain.

I won't defend what the governor did, but it could

have turned out way worse for the moron with the SUV. He could have ended up in a hospital like Dodge Olney. Instead his vehicle was the only thing that got hurt.

You don't need to be a trained mechanic to know that gasoline engines won't run on water, barley malt, hops, rice and yeast, which are the basic ingredients of Budweiser beer. I Googled it while hunkered low in the Malibu.

Skink knelt by the blue SUV and calmly poured an entire six-pack into the fuel tank. Then, just to make sure his message was received, he jammed the empties up the tailpipe. I was praying that nobody in the restaurant could see what was happening through the downpour.

Once we were back on Highway 19, I sat upright and told the governor he was crazy. "What were you thinking? I mean it!"

"Litterbugs are the lowest." His clothes were sopping, his shower cap spangled with raindrops.

"What happens if you get thrown in jail?" I was pretty upset. "Am I supposed to go save Malley all by myself?"

"There's some beautiful country up in this part of the state. I see some jackass trashing it, I can't turn away."

The governor's glass eye had fogged, but of course he didn't know it. Earlier I'd asked him why he didn't get a green one to match his real one. He said that the brown eye came from a stuffed bear (which is why it didn't fit properly in his semi-human skull). He'd never, ever harm a bear, he said. Bears carry heavy mojo. The taxidermied specimen belonged to some fool who fancied himself a big-game hunter. Skink had gone to visit the hunter on a "non-social visit." His words.

After calming down, I said, "What you just did back there was a crime. You totaled that dude's engine."

"He might coax a mile or two out of it."

"What if they had security cameras in the parking lot?"

"In Homosassa, Florida? Ha!"

Trying to reason with him was hopeless.

"Friend of mine," he said, "once emptied a loaded Dumpster into a BMW convertible. Same basic scenario—driver had thrown all his Burger King bags out on the turnpike."

"I get why you're mad. It makes me mad, too, but—"

"We are who we are."

"Yeah, whatever," I said.

Beth called again. She'd gotten a text from Malley and it was, like, la-de-da, T.C. is so awesome, etc. I told Beth I was heading upstate on a hunch, and I'd check back in a few days. She kept on talking. Honestly, I didn't really want to hear about her problems with her boyfriend, Taylor. All he cared about was baseball, she said. Plus he was a lame dancer. I hardly knew Taylor, but I had no interest in getting between him and Beth. Once she dumped him, different story.

Skink was pretending not to listen as I worked my way out of the conversation. After the call was over, I shrugged and said, "Hey, she's just a friend."

"I've had a few of those." He scratched at his beard. "How's your mother holding up?"

I opened my laptop and read her email aloud. It was part-mom, part-lawyer:

Dear Richard,

I intended to say all this in a phone call, but sometimes it's easier to sort my thoughts when I put them in writing.

You understand why I'm not enthusiastic about this impulsive trip of yours. We're all worried about your cousin, but my job is to worry about you. I spoke at length with the mysterious "Mr. Tile," and in confidence he gave me the history of the gentleman with whom you're traveling. He said that this person, despite his age, was physically capable of protecting you from any harm, and that he wouldn't hesitate to give up his own life in your defense, if necessary.

It would be untrue to say that I wasn't comforted by Mr. Tile's assurances. I did a little research of my own, which confirmed the basic biographical details about this "Skink" individual. However, I also came across accounts of certain incidents that I can only pray have been exaggerated by legend. If even half the stories are true, he clearly isn't the most stable of companions. Please, please be careful.

Mr. Tile has promised to stay in contact, but I'm still very apprehensive about this road trip you've embarked upon. Personally, I don't believe Malley can be found if she doesn't wish to be, or that she necessarily needs to be "rescued." Her phone calls home have been fairly breezy and lighthearted, according to Dan and Sandy. Based on past experiences, I'm betting she'll be back in Loggerhead Beach as soon as she gets bored with this latest escapade.

Obviously you believe she might be in danger, and if that's true, then you could be in danger, too. Again I'm asking you to back off and let the authorities handle this. There's nothing you and "Skink" can do that couldn't be done more safely by experienced law-enforcement officers. Honestly, it's only because of Mr. Tile that I haven't called the police myself and put out an Amber Alert for you!

At times like this I find myself wondering what your father would do if he were here. As you know, he was always the "free spirit" in our family. He used to tell me it was healthy to let you boys cut loose and take a few chances, but I suspect that even he would be alarmed by what you're doing.

Please come home, honey.

Love always,
Mom

I shut the computer and looked at the governor to see if he was offended by my mother's suggestion that he might be a psycho.

All he said was: "You're a lucky young man."

"I know."

"You want to go home, that's cool."

"It's not like I want to. But—"

"Something happens to you, she'll be shattered."

"That's why I quit surfing after Dad died," I said. "My brothers—they're just insane on the water. No fear. Mom can't even watch."

"You're the one she depends on to always be there. The steady son, right?"

"Something like that."

Outside, the rain had let up. The Malibu's windshield wipers squeaked on the glass. One of Skink's songs was playing on the sound system. *Help me, Rhonda. Help, help me, Rhonda.*

He said, "There's an airport in Bay County. Have her call and line up a flight to Orlando. I'd put you on a Greyhound bus, but you might wind up sitting next to somebody who looks worse than me."

"Why can't I just ride back with you in the car?"

"Because I'm not going back."

"Oh." At first I didn't catch on.

"I'm going to find your cousin," he said.

And that was that. With or without my help, the old man aimed to track down Malley and take her away from the Talbo Chock impostor.

A few hours later, as the sun disappeared through a frill of fluffy pink clouds, we stood along Massalina Bayou in downtown Panama City. The Tarpon Dock drawbridge was rising for a shrimp boat coming in from the Gulf. Above its stern swirled a confetti of gulls and terns, crying hungrily. The boat captain sounded his horn.

My shoulders were shaking, I was so amped. "This must be it! The bridge she called me from!"

The shrimper was eyeing us from the cockpit as his boat rumbled past. Skink pulled off his shower cap and shoved it inside a pocket. The gash on his scalp was purple from iodine, and I could see a cross-hatching of black threads. He must have pulled the car over and stitched himself up while I was asleep.

"So, what'd you tell your mom?" he asked.

"I told her I trusted you."

The governor smiled. "Does that mean you don't want a ride to the airport?"

"No airport," I said.

"Outstanding." He unknotted his snake-rattle necklace and presented it to me.

I wish I still had it.

EIGHT

Scientists search for ivory-billed woodpeckers with the same fanatic determination that some people hunt for Bigfoots.

The difference is that those woodpeckers were real. They lived in old hardwood forests throughout the southeastern United States until after the Civil War, when the timber industry moved in and started chopping down millions of trees. Eventually the birds had no more bark beetles to eat, no old dead trunks for pecking out their nest holes. Once it became known that ivorybills were disappearing, they were stalked and shot by hunters who sold the bodies to museums, so that they could be stuffed and put on display like dinosaurs. Pitiful but true.

The woodpecker was crazy beautiful—tall and long-beaked, with pale yellow eyes and bluish-black feathers. Bright white streaks ran down each side of its neck, spreading to the wings. The bird's most striking feature was a sharp crest on the back of its head—black for females, bright red for males. The ivorybill's appearance was so dramatic that it was nicknamed the "Lord God Bird," because "Lord God!" is what people supposedly exclaimed when they first saw one.

There hasn't been a one hundred percent documented encounter with the species in something like eighty years. Random sightings are reported, but, like Bigfoot, not a single ivorybill has been positively located and identified. What people often see (and get excited about) is really a pileated woodpecker, which also has a vivid red crest. That bird is smaller, though, with brownish feathers and a shorter beak. It also has less white on the wing markings.

I know all this from doing my science fair project, which won an honorable mention at school. I wouldn't call myself an ivorybill expert, but I did a ton of research. Because ivorybills vanished so long ago, no color photographs of the birds exist. Malley helped me draw a likeness on my poster board. To be accurate, we studied century-old illustrations and also a painting of three ivorybills by John James Audubon, the famous nature artist who spent lots of time in Florida.

Unfortunately, Audubon usually shot the species he wanted to paint, in order to examine them up close. This was back in the 1820s, when there were still plenty of ivorybills around, but I bet today he'd trade that painting for a glimpse of a live one. The last known population was wiped out in the 1930s when a Chicago lumber company clear-cut an ancient Louisiana forest. Lots of folks, even some politicians, pleaded with the loggers not to saw down those trees, but the company refused to stop.

And with that, the ivory-billed woodpecker became a ghost. In Florida the legend lives on in the deep woods along the Choctawhatchee River, which winds down into the Panhandle from southern Alabama. Malley also worked with me on my habitat map. That's how she was able to get on the phone and tell me where she was without alerting the fake Talbo Chock. All she had to say was that she'd heard an ivorybill. Only a bird geek like me would put two and two together.

Not so long ago, researchers from two big-time universities published a study listing fourteen reliable sightings of the ivorybill in the Choctawhatchee basin, as well as three hundred recordings of distinct calls and bark drumming known to be made by the elusive woodpecker. However, after several years of trying, no scientist or civilian has been able to produce clear photographic evidence of a living specimen along that river—or anywhere else in the United States.

A famous video that supposedly shows an ivorybill flying in an Arkansas swamp was rejected by top ornithologists, who said the bird was most likely a pileated woodpecker. I included a YouTube clip of that video in my science fair project, which was interactive. People could touch a button and hear a recording that compared the different hammering patterns of the pileated and the ivory-billed. I re-created the sounds myself by tapping a hollow bamboo reed against a dead palm tree.

It would be awesome if someone actually discovered

a live ivorybill, but that hasn't happened. The bird is officially classified as extinct, and that's what I concluded in my project. They're all gone.

"Don't be so sure," the governor said.

"Now you sound like my stepfather. He totally believes in Sasquatches."

"I saw one of those woodpeckers with my own eye."

"Right," I said.

"April 17, 2009. Tomorrow I'll show you where."

Choctawhatchee Bay, where the river empties, is only a short drive from Panama City, but Skink decided to wait until morning to begin our search for Malley. He said snooping around after dark was too risky. In the daylight hours we could pose as grandfather and grandson on a lazy summer road trip.

"Don't you have, like, a regular hat?" I asked.

He smoothed the wrinkles from his shower cap and sourly jabbed a stick into the embers of the fire. We were camping in piney scrub near a place called Ebro. The governor was frying two dozen oysters he'd bought at a fish house and shucked with a combat knife. I'd never been brave enough to eat an oyster, but I agreed to try one because my other option was boiled roadkill. Skink had scavenged a dead raccoon on Highway 98. It had been struck by a vehicle with extremely large tires, and the furry ringed tail was the only way you could tell what kind of mammal it was.

The oysters actually were tasty, and I ended up eating

more than the governor did. After we finished, he gathered up the empty shells and went off to bury them. That's when my mother called.

"Where are you?" she asked. "I've got a road map of Florida in front of me."

"I can't tell you, but we're definitely getting close to Malley."

"Hold on. Did you really just say you can't tell me?"

"I promised him I wouldn't give out too much information."

"By 'him,' you mean Mr. Tyree. Has he legally adopted you now? Because, if not, I'm still the one responsible for your health and well-being!"

"Okay, Mom. Okay." I told her we were camping in the Panhandle. She asked for the name of the nearest city, and I said we were somewhere west of Tallahassee.

"Oh, that's a tremendous help, Richard. You might as well have said east of Mobile."

"Mom, everything's fine. We had fresh oysters for dinner, okay? It's not like I'm suffering. He's got bug spray, blankets, soap, even a snakebite kit."

Dumb mistake on my part, mentioning the snakebite kit.

"Oh, great. So you're in a wild swamp," my mother sighed, "with moccasins and rattlers."

"We are *not* in a swamp. You gotta chill, please?"

"Has he done anything crazy yet? Tell the truth."

"He cussed at some litterbug on the highway," I said.

"That's not crazy—you do the same thing." Except my mother has never poured beer into another driver's gas tank, no matter what stupid thing he's done.

Trent got on the line to say how disappointed he was in me for lying about going camping with Blake. I apologized for getting him into trouble with Mom.

He said, "Best thing you could do, bro, is beam yourself home ASAP."

"Not just yet."

"Let the cops find Malley. What are you—like, mister secret agent bounty hunter?"

The difference was that bounty hunters chase down people to get the reward money; I was tracking my cousin because I was worried about her.

"Trent, can I please talk to Mom again?"

There was a muffled exchange of the phone, then my mother's tense voice: "Richard, if you do find Malley, I want your word that you and Mr. Tyree won't do anything reckless. Just hang back and call the police, all right? Don't try to be heroes."

"Of course," I said, knowing the governor was out of my control. He couldn't wait to have a "chat" with the fake Talbo.

"Also," Mom added, "you've got exactly seventy-two hours."

"Why? Then what?"

"Then I'll be notifying the authorities."

"But what about Mr. Tile—"

"I'll be telling him the same thing," she said. "Three days from now I expect to see your smiling, unharmed face in this house. If you're not back by then, I'm basically calling out the cavalry."

"Mom, come on!"

"That's the deal, Richard. Now, may I speak to Governor Tyree, or Skink, or whatever he's calling himself?"

"Uh, he stepped away."

"Stepped away? To where? Don't tell me he left you alone out there—"

"Later, Mom."

The reason I clicked off in such a hurry was that I heard a truck honking and a high-pitched scrape of brakes out on the road, not far from our campfire. Using the flashlight app, I picked my way through the woods, not even trying to be quiet.

By the time I reached the road, the truck was out of sight. Shards of oyster shells littered the pavement. I called out for the governor, sweeping my little flashlight back and forth. The glow fell upon a boot, an exceptionally large boot, standing empty on the gravel shoulder. I saw that the toe of the boot had been crushed, practically flattened. A grimy, torn sock lay crumpled nearby.

When I yelled again, my voice cracked.

A froggy reply came out of the darkness:

"Over here, son." Followed by a gusher of swear words. I aimed the light toward a ditch, and that's where he was sprawled. His bare right foot looked crooked and pulpy.

"What happened?" I cried.

"I'm not as quick as I used to be, that's what happened. Here, hold this."

"No way!" It was a baby skunk, and I didn't have to look twice to be sure. A skunk the size of a guinea pig but still a skunk, stripes and all.

"Do what I say," Skink growled. "Stay calm and she won't spray. And kill that freaking light."

So I cradled the little stinker in the crook of my arm while the governor gimped out of the ditch and retrieved his boot, which no longer fit over his mangled toes. The skunk didn't make a sound, but I could feel it tremble.

"We are *not* eating her," I said.

"Don't be a nitwit, Richard. If I'd wanted to eat her, we wouldn't be having this discussion."

Turned out that the baby skunk had been crossing the road behind its mother when an eighteen-wheeler came speeding down the hill. Skunks have poor eyesight, so they never saw what was coming. The momma made it safely to the other side but the small one was too slow. The governor had dropped the oyster shells, dashed into the road, snatched up the youngster and then tried to leap out of the way. The truck missed everything but his right foot.

Now he was limping ahead of me through the trees. I didn't need the flashlight app to see which way he was going—I just followed the ripe smell of oysters. He was looking for the mother skunk, and somehow he tracked her down. It was impressive. He said she wouldn't spray us with musk if we talked softly, and she didn't. He took the little skunk from me and set her on the ground. The critter was so blind that he had to spin her around until she was pointed toward the mother. Off they went, two black bushy tails trundling single-file through the scrub.

The governor was in a world of pain, grunting and cussing as he hopped along. I found a sturdy stick for him to use as a walking cane, but he was still breathing hard and shiny with sweat by the time we reached the road.

"Damn polecats," he grumbled. "Richard, there's a well-known saying: 'No good deed goes unpunished.'"

"Don't you believe in karma? I do."

"You're not the one walkin' on broken bones."

A pair of low-set headlights appeared at the top of the hill. It was definitely a car, not a truck, and it was approaching at high speed. Skink told me to get in the ditch and stay down. I asked why.

"In case it's the sheriff or a game warden," he said impatiently. "I don't feel like tryin' to explain what we're doing out here in the boonies in the dead of night. Once they see my run-over foot, they'll call an ambulance and send me straight to Emergency."

"Well, that's where you need to be."

He gave me a push toward the ditch. "No detours, son. We've got work to do." He slid down beside me, removing his shower cap so that the oncoming lights wouldn't catch the shine of the plastic.

The car was easily doing sixty as it sped past, but we peeked up just in time for a glimpse. It wasn't a police cruiser. It was a light-colored Toyota.

"That a Camry?" Skink asked. "Or a Corolla?"

"I couldn't tell. It was going way too fast."

"I didn't get a look at the rear windshield. You see a pellet hole?"

"No, it was going too fast," I said again. The only thing I saw clearly was the chrome logo on the trunk—a circle with two small ovals linked crossways inside. I recognized it because my father once had a Toyota minivan.

Skink said this model was definitely a two-door. "That's what we're lookin' for, right?"

"Yep." I was ready to jump out of my skin, I was so excited.

The governor struggled upright and got himself back out on the road. "Northbound," he muttered, peering at the vanishing taillights. "Maybe you're right about that baby skunk. Maybe she brought us some luck."

I stood beside him on the center line wondering if I was watching my cousin fade out of sight, and out of reach. "Then hurry, let's go!" I practically shouted. "Come on! You make a splint while I douse the fire and pack our stuff."

He laughed ruefully. "Sounds like a fine plan, Richard, except for one small problem."

"What now?"

"You know how to drive?"

"Of course I don't. I'm not old enough."

"Lesson number one." Skink waggled his smashed boot in the air. "It's the right foot that goes back and forth between the gas pedal and the brake."

"Oh God." I felt like throwing up. "Can't you do it lefty?"

"Too tricky," he explained. "Plus I'm in a severe amount of discomfort. Mr. Tile always keeps proper medicine in the first-aid kit, but it'll leave me unfit to operate heavy machinery."

"Like a Chevy Malibu."

"Correct." The governor hobbled back through the woods toward our campfire. I stepped ahead of him, lighting the way with my LED.

"What if Malley was in that car?" I asked miserably. "We can't just sit around here roasting s'mores until your stupid foot gets better."

"No, son. We continue the pursuit." Every step caused him to wince.

"But we can't go anywhere if you're too crippled to drive."

"From now on you'll be our driver, Richard. I'll teach you how."

"Tonight? No way. In the dark? I don't think I can deal with that."

"Relax," he said. "The highways of this state are teeming with mental defectives."

"Gee, thanks."

"All I'm saying is anyone can do it."

"I could get arrested—underage, with no license! Mom would go totally ballistic if I had to call her from jail."

"Nobody in this vehicle will be getting arrested." Skink stated this as a concrete fact.

I wasn't scared of trying to drive a car, but I was nervous. Supernervous, to be honest. The circumstances weren't exactly ideal.

Broad daylight in the empty parking lot of a football stadium? No problem. Pitch-black night on a winding country road? Different story.

From behind I felt a friendly poke from the governor's walking stick.

"You'll do fine," he said. "I'll even let you put on your own music."

NINE

My height is an issue.

Dad was five foot eleven. Kyle's five ten and Robbie is six feet even. Uncle Dan is six one even, and Mom's five nine.

I stand only five feet one and a half inches tall—still waiting on my growth spurt, hormones, whatever. My legs are fairly long, but the rest of me is waiting to catch up.

Bottom line: From the bucket seat it was a stretch to see over the steering wheel. For my first driving lesson I wanted perfect 360-degree vision. What I needed was something to sit on.

Skink told me to check the trunk. It was packed with books, which is not what I'd expected. There was other stuff, too—pots, pans, clothes, batteries, sleeping bags, a fishing rod, a gun case—but his books took up most of the space. I picked out two of the fattest hardbacks. The first was *East of Eden*, a novel by John Steinbeck. The second was *The Oxford English Dictionary*, volume one.

I stacked them on the driver's seat and got myself

centered on top. It was like sitting on a throne with sharp edges.

"Don't fart on my Steinbeck," the governor warned, "or you're toast."

"Now I'm too tall to reach the brake."

"Then lose the dictionary." He jerked it out from under me. "You ready, King Richard?"

"Not really."

"Buckle up."

The only motorized vehicle I'd ever driven was a golf cart, courtesy of my stepfather. He lets me take the wheel whenever we go to the course because he likes to ride shotgun. That way his hands are free to text and guzzle his Mountain Dew. The carts at Trent's club are set up like cars—the steering wheel is on the left side, and the brake pedal is in the same place in relation to the accelerator. The big difference between a golf cart and an automobile is that a golf cart won't go ninety miles an hour unless you drive it off a cliff.

Skink was sitting beside me, wrapping his pulverized foot with an Ace bandage. He reached over and twisted the key in the ignition. The dashboard panel lit up like a jet cockpit. I could feel the soft vibration of the Malibu's engine through the soles of my sneakers.

"Turn on the headlights," he said.

"Which way should I go?"

"Let's start with straight ahead."

I was so stressed that I was basically strangling the steering wheel.

"Put her in Drive," the governor advised.

When my foot met the accelerator, the car lurched forward and I yelled a word that my mother wouldn't have appreciated.

Skink just laughed. "Easy there, boy. Pretend there's an egg under the pedal."

We stayed on the dirt logging road near our camp. It was a jolting, dusty ride, but at least there were no sharp curves to deal with. Back and forth I went—my top speed was twenty-five, maybe thirty. Every so often the governor would tell me to hit the brakes, hard. Pretty soon I had a good feel for how the Chevy responded.

Backing up for the turnarounds was challenging— the first few times, we ended up with the taillights in the bushes. "Try again," Skink would say.

He never once yelled at me, which I appreciated. The whole time behind the wheel I kept thinking about what Mom would say if she could see me. My father, too. He was what you might call a casual driver. Totally laid-back, which was okay on beach streets but not so much on Interstate 95. One time he nearly killed the whole family because he was gazing at a dragon-shaped cloud instead of at the semi that was broken down in the lane dead ahead of us. After that bit of excitement, my mother became the designated driver on all our vacations.

It was past midnight when I parked the Chevy and

we returned to the campsite. Skink tossed me a sleeping bag but stretched out on the open ground near the fire. Within minutes he was snoring. I checked my phone for new emails, but there was nothing from Malley. She was still communicating strictly by phone, and not very often.

I lay down and replayed in my head the fleeting sight of that white Toyota. Sometimes your mind absorbs more details than you realize. Yet as hard as I tried—and as much as I *wanted* it to be the right car—I just couldn't re-create the visual of a small gunshot hole in the rear windshield. Maybe the pellet damage was there, maybe it wasn't. Maybe the car was a Camry, maybe a Corolla.

And maybe the driver was returning to a secret hiding place in woodpecker country, or maybe he was just heading to a business meeting in Alabama.

Trying to sleep was hopeless. Somewhere deep in the trees a pair of screech owls called back and forth, like two lovesick horses whinnying. A jumbo-sized moth flitted in and out of the firelight. The first time I saw it, I thought it was a bat and covered my head.

After a while the embers turned to ash and stopped crackling. The only sound was Skink's snoring, which gradually morphed into whimpers and then snarls. I wondered if the pain from his broken foot was giving him a nightmare, or if it was something left over from Vietnam. In school we'd read about what terrible combat experiences can do to a soldier—post-traumatic stress disorder, they call it.

Part of me wanted to wake him and tell him everything was all right, and part of me was afraid to touch him in case he went berserk. Gently I nudged him with his walking stick, and sure enough, he began thrashing wildly like he was suffering some kind of seizure. I grabbed the phone from my backpack to dial 911 when he just as suddenly fell still.

Panting, he blinked open his good eye.

"You okay?" I asked.

He coughed hard and nodded.

"What were you dreaming about?"

"Lollipops," he grunted. "Lollipops and butterflies."

"Was it the war?" I handed him a bottle of water.

"'A dream has power to poison sleep.' That's from a poet named Shelley. He's worth a read." Skink rose slowly and dusted himself off. "What time is it, Richard?"

"Late."

We sat up talking. He told me about two friends who'd died fighting with him in Vietnam, and I told him about my father. We agreed that it sucked to lose somebody you love at a young age.

"How'd you get nicknamed after a lizard?" I asked.

He laughed. "Pure Jim Tile. One time he got mad at me and said I was slippery as a skink. Apparently it stuck."

I told him I'd once caught a five-lined skink in a log pile, though it hadn't been easy. They do have shiny slick skin, and sneaky moves. "Plus they bite," I added.

"Like all survivors." He unwound the bandage from his foot and scowled at the sight. "There goes my soccer career."

"What's the plan for the morning?" I asked.

"Head north and scout the river. If they're camping out, they'll be near water."

"Won't we need a boat?"

"Dumb luck," said Skink, "is what we need."

He snapped off a couple of stout branches and fashioned a splint for his lower leg. I helped him rewrap the Ace bandage until it was supertight. He used his knife to slice his smashed boot into a crude sandal, which he fit over his injured foot.

The night air was warm enough that we didn't need the fire. Neither of us could fall sleep. I think Skink was afraid of tumbling back into the same nightmare—and I wanted to stay wide awake in case he did.

Using the walking stick, he went to the car and picked two books from the trunk. The one he handed to me was called *Silent Spring*, by Rachel Carson. It was an exposé about a horrible pesticide called DDT and other man-made chemicals, which killed off bald eagles and lots of other wildlife. I'd seen the book before. My mother kept a copy displayed on a shelf behind the desk in her law office. Skink said it was a classic.

"They didn't make you read this in school? That's disgraceful!" he boomed.

I turned on my LED pen and opened to the first chapter. He settled in by the smoky ashes and took out a regular flashlight. The book he'd chosen was *Grizzly Years*, by a man named Doug Peacock, who the governor said was a medic he'd met in Vietnam. The war was so hard on Mr. Peacock that he came back and disappeared into the mountains of Wyoming and Montana, where he lived for many years among wild grizzly bears. He didn't take a gun along, either. True story. I felt like asking Skink if we could trade books, but I didn't want to aggravate him.

And, to be honest, *Silent Spring* was a good read. It came out back in 1962, before my father was born, but even half a century later, reading it will make you angry. Skink told me that DDT was basically outlawed after the book was published, which was an epic victory. He also said there are plenty of other chemicals that are just as bad and totally legal.

Nobody spoke again until an hour or so before sunrise, when a deer wandered up to the camp. "Hello, you," I said, and it dashed off.

Darkness gave way to a soft golden glow in the east. For breakfast the governor poured some granola mix into a pan, and we ate it dry.

My phone went off, the first whale song ever heard in those woods.

"Malley?"

"Hey, it's me." She was half mumbling.

"You're up early. Can you talk?"

"Not at all."

"Tell me whatever you can."

"Nothing, Mom," she said. "Everything's awesome."

I could hear a male voice in the background. Obviously she'd told Online Talbo that she was calling her mother.

"If you need help," I said, "ask me about your dad."

"Sure. How's Dad doing?"

I looked at the governor, who moved his fingers like he was pulling on a piece of taffy. String out the conversation, he was telling me. Get more information.

"If you're still in Florida," I said to Malley, "say something about the weather."

"It's been sunny and clear, just fantastic. You guys had rain?"

By now I was cupping the phone with both hands. "This is important, Mal. Are you still at that ivorybill place?"

"Yeah, I saw one up in the tree this morning!" she said lightly.

"The Choctawhatchee River, right? Like on the map we did for my project?"

"Absolutely, Mom. I miss you, too, but this is, like, the best trip ever. Off-the-hook amazing!"

"Listen to me," I whispered. "I'm coming to get you."

"That's so sweet."

Skink motioned for me to cover the phone. "Ask if

she's north or south of the bridge on State Road 20. Then find out how far."

"Mal, there's a bridge on Road 20," I said to her.

"I know, Mom."

"Say 'sardines' if you're north of there. Say 'clams' if you're south."

"Clams. And they looked delicious."

"How far? Say something besides miles. Rainbows, hiccups, I don't know . . ."

"Otters," she said. "Yesterday I saw two of 'em."

"Got it, Mal. Two miles south of the bridge."

Then the voice in the background said: "Hang up, damn it!"

And she did.

We rolled out at dawn. The traffic was zero. Driving on the pavement was smoother than on the logging road, and way quieter.

"Faster, Richard," said Skink.

I was perched with my butt on the Steinbeck novel, my eyes jumping back and forth between the road and the dashboard gauges. When the speedometer reached fifty, the governor raised a hand.

"Is this good?" I asked.

"Fabulous." He sounded groggy, which concerned me.

"Did you take one of those pain pills?"

"I'm sharp as a tack, sport."

"Good, 'cause I can't do this alone."

"What's the speed limit out here?" he asked.

"The sign said fifty-five."

"Very sensible."

"I'd really like to keep it at fifty."

"You're a model citizen, Richard. Fifty it is."

True to his promise, Skink plugged my iPod into the car's sound system. I expected some harsh commentary, but he actually liked several artists on my playlist. His favorites were the Black Keys and Jack Johnson. When Adele came on, he shrugged and said no woman on the planet ever sang better than Linda Ronstadt. He spelled the last name for me, and I promised to check her out. When I played a cut by Skrillex, he covered his ears and started moaning like a sick baboon.

We were heading the same direction as the mystery Toyota, and my driving was smooth and steady. Then we came up behind a truck, and that's when I got the shakes. It was a tall brown UPS delivery truck, the same kind my father had crashed into on his skateboard. An awful thought wormed into my head:

This is the last sight Dad ever saw.

I must have gone pale, because Skink asked what was wrong. My hands were locked on the steering wheel and my eyes were riveted on the UPS logo. I wasn't tailgating or anything, but I was definitely in a weird half-hypnotized mode.

The governor told me to pass the truck. The road had

four lanes, two going each way. Plenty of room to scoot by on the left.

"Can't do it," I said.

"Then pull over and take a break."

"No, I'm okay." Untrue.

The accident had totally been my father's fault. The UPS truck had been parked by a curb with its flashers on. The driver, who felt the impact, jumped out of the cab to run back and help. Nothing could be done for Dad, of course. A police officer called Mom, and she got there ten minutes later. I was in school, thank God. She never talked to me and my brothers about what that scene was like, but it must have been brutal. I still have a dream where I'm there, too, trying to climb into the back of the ambulance so I can ride with my father to the hospital— except the ambulance doors won't open, no matter how hard I pull. I always wake up soaked with sweat and gasping for air.

For like a year after he died, my mother wouldn't order anything from Amazon, because in our neighborhood all the Amazon shipments are delivered by UPS. Every time Mom saw one of those brown trucks, she'd start crying. Now she's over that and back to her crazy online shopping, and UPS comes to our house all the time. It had never bothered me—at least I didn't think it had.

"Tell me what's wrong," Skink said.

"Nothing."

"The snake rattle you're wearing around your neck? It has eighteen buttons."

"Yeah, so?"

"That was a big-ass reptile, son. A button for every year of its life. You want to make it to age eighteen, or you want to break your momma's heart?"

I was in a hot woozy fog. It felt like the car was driving *me,* not the other way around.

"Look behind us," he said.

"Oh great."

A dark sedan was on our tail, a bright blue light flashing on its dashboard.

"What now?" I asked blankly.

"Calmly remove your foot from the accelerator and place it on the brake pedal."

It wasn't the smoothest stop in the history of automotive travel, but I managed to guide the Malibu safely to the shoulder of the road. As soon as the UPS truck disappeared from view, I snapped out of my brainless daze. In the mirror I saw the officer stepping out of the unmarked police car.

"Highway Patrol," the governor said.

Anxiously I turned to him. "Sorry, but I can't lie about this. Not to a cop."

"I understand."

Now the trooper loomed at my window. He was tall and heavyset. Like Detective Trujillo, he wore plain clothes—tan slacks and a Nike golf shirt, the same brand that Trent buys. A gold badge was clipped to his belt, a small blunt-nosed gun holstered on his hip.

I was too nervous to make eye contact, so I stared idiotically at my knuckles on the steering wheel.

"Officer, was I speeding?"

"Not at all."

"This isn't my car."

Skink sighed. "He knows that."

"Look, I'm really sorry," I blurted, "but I don't have a driver's license."

"You do now," the trooper said.

He handed me a laminated card stamped with holograms of the Florida state seal. It was a real learner's permit, with my real name and photo—the same one from my middle-school yearbook. My home address was on the license, along with my height and weight. Every detail was correct except the date of my birth, which was off by exactly one year.

That wasn't a random mistake. It made me legally old enough to operate a motor vehicle with an adult riding in the passenger seat.

"Someone found it by the bridge in Panama City," said the trooper.

I sat wordless, studying the shiny card.

Skink was smiling. "Must've fallen out of his backpack. Thank you, officer."

The man leaned over and looked into the car. He

was an African American, and way old enough to be retired from the state police. His hair was white as a glacier, though his arms were like ship cables.

"Safe travels, gentlemen," he said.

The governor winked at him and thundered: "Brother, you restore my faith in humanity!"

"I doubt that." The man put on his sunglasses. "Richard, you keep a close eye on this old fart."

A minute later the sedan was gone, a dark speck vanishing in the distance. I slipped my new driver's license into a back pocket and turned the key in the Malibu.

"That was him, right?"

"Who?" said Skink.

"Your friend Mr. Tile."

"Can you believe he called me an old fart?"

TEN

The Choctawhatchee River was wide and sleepy-looking. We stood on the Road 20 bridge gazing down at the brown water, swollen by hard summer rains. Lush trees lined the banks, and a pair of ospreys coasted back and forth searching for mullets.

"Mom says we've got three days and then she's calling the cops."

"Ha! Plenty of time," the governor said.

A large fish made a splash by the pilings, and Skink declared it was a sturgeon. "They jump like lunatics during mating season. One of 'em demolished a Jet Ski a few years back. *That* I'd pay to see."

"You sure this is the right place?"

"I am." He was peering down at something, shielding his good eye from the sun. "Stay here," he told me.

"Where are you going?"

"For a dip."

With surprising agility he crossed to the end of the span and descended a steep grassy slope toward the base of the bridge. For a few moments I lost sight of him among the concrete pillars. When he emerged, I noticed that he'd removed his leg splint and kicked off both his boots.

Into the river he went, and that's when I saw what he'd seen—a long whitish shape on the bottom. The angled light gave it a hazed, spooky glow.

I hurried down to the shoreline, but I was too freaked to jump in after him. "Useless" is the word for it. I actually turned away and threw up.

The governor dove three, four, five times. Whenever his head popped to the surface, he sounded like a creaky old manatee sucking air. I folded into a heap on the ground and waited for the sky to stop spinning. It was more than fear that paralyzed me; it was pure dread.

Skink sloshed out of the river, panting. His hair was slicked and his silver beard glistened.

I practically choked on the question: "Is that it?"

"Yep."

"You check the license tag?"

"Tag's been yanked off."

"Is . . . is she—?"

"Nobody's inside, son. Not a soul."

"You're a hundred percent sure it's the same one? Did you look at the back windshield?"

"There is a pellet hole. There's also a big rock on the accelerator."

He located the tire tracks where the bogus Talbo Chock had sent the stolen Toyota rolling into the

Choctawhatchee. Now the submerged car was obscured by a milky cloud of mud, stirred by Skink's explorations.

"But you didn't see Malley?" I asked in a thick voice. "You'd tell me if she was down there, right?"

"I'd have her in my arms right now."

"What about the trunk? You look in there?" It made me sick to think about it, but I had to know.

"I popped the trunk," Skink said patiently. "Nothing but a spare tire and some soggy Bibles. The preacher's stash, no doubt."

"So Malley's still alive!"

"My guess is they got a boat."

Which meant they were probably moving downriver. If they were two miles from the bridge at dawn, when Malley called, they could be much farther now. It all depended on where the fake Talbo intended to go, and how fast. Maybe he was just searching for a place to hide on the river.

"We need a boat, too," I said, "like *immediately*."

The governor smiled and extended a dripping arm toward the ramp on the downriver side of the bridge. There a middle-aged man and woman were carefully lifting an aluminum canoe off the top of their minivan.

"That," Skink said, "is what you call destiny."

"So, those people are just going to loan us their canoe? Two total strangers."

"Of course not."

"Please don't tell me we're going to steal it."

"This is not the movies, Richard. There's a shoe box in the back of the car. Please go get it while I take a long, glorious leak."

The couple was Mr. and Mrs. Capps, from Thomasville, Georgia. At first they were rattled by the strange vision of the governor lurching their way, but before long he charmed them into believing that he was my grandfather. He said we were on a camping trip but that some jerk stole our kayak down in Apalachicola.

"Richard was devastated," Skink said. "Right, buddy?"

I tried my best to look devastated.

Mrs. Capps patted my shoulder and said it was a cold rotten world if people went around swiping kids' watercrafts.

"So true," Skink agreed with a frown. "I tried to stop the thug but he whacked me on the skull with a crowbar and then ran over my foot with his station wagon."

He displayed his impressive injuries to Mr. Capps and his wife, who were outraged. They asked if we'd called the police and I said yes, of course, but the bad guy still got away. That was my only contribution to the governor's made-up story.

"Folks, here's the situation," he went on. "This is probably our very last river trip together, me and Richard. I'm not gettin' any younger and, well, last time I went in the hospital the MRI didn't look so peachy. It's my lungs."

Naturally, Mr. and Mrs. Capps took this to mean that the cockeyed old man was deathly ill.

"I'm so sorry," said Mr. Capps.

Except it turned out he was actually *Doctor* Capps, and he started pressing Skink for details about his medical condition. From the governor's mumbling, it was obvious that he hadn't thought up an actual disease for himself, so I piped up and said, "Gramps's got emphysema."

Which is a rough deal, I know. One of my great-aunts had it. She'd smoked four packs of cigarettes a day for thirty years, and her insides looked like a tar pit. That's Malley's description, not mine.

"Oh my," said Mrs. Capps.

Skink manufactured a sad, sickly cough. "Bottom line, I was wondering if you'd be kind enough to sell us your canoe."

Dr. Capps looked reluctant. "Gosh, I don't know," he said. "It's been in the family for years."

The governor displayed a roll of cash that he'd taken from the shoe box. The bills were moist and dirty, and for all I knew they'd been buried in a graveyard.

He held out the money. "Here's a thousand dollars. That's how much this trip with my grandson means to me."

I'm not sure whose jaw dropped farther, mine or the doctor's.

"Please take it," said Skink.

"Well . . ."

One of Dr. Capps's hands began to reach for the wad, but his wife slapped it down, saying, "John, that's way, *way* too much! We bought that old canoe from your brother for only—"

"Grace, I'll handle this."

"For heaven's sake, where's your heart?"

I didn't make a peep. I was still trying to get my head around the fact that we'd been driving around Florida with a shoe box full of money like a couple of dope smugglers.

"How about five hundred?" the doctor said.

"Done." The governor slowly peeled off the bills—twenty-five twenties.

Mrs. Capps's objections seemed to fade at the sight of all that money, though she worked hard to maintain a compassionate attitude. "Oh dear, what's wrong with your eye?" she asked Skink.

His left socket was leaking some sort of gross fluid that dribbled down into his beard.

"I know some excellent ophthalmologists," offered Dr. Capps, "if you need a referral."

"Least of my problems," said Skink.

He pried out the fake eye and threw it into the river, where it disappeared with a plop. From a small soiled satchel he selected a replacement. This one had a sky-blue iris and was shaped more like half a clam than a marble. With difficulty (and a few cuss words) the governor inserted the glass piece into the pulpy crater under his brow.

"It's an antique," he explained matter-of-factly, blinking away the ooze.

Mortified, the doctor and his wife clambered into

their minivan and sped off in a hail of gravel. We carried the canoe to the water and began loading our gear. Skink laughed when I asked if we should bring the gun case. He sprung the latches and took out an ancient golf club with a peeling leather grip.

"Nine-iron," he said, tossing it aboard the canoe. "Inside joke. Mr. Tile doesn't trust me with firearms."

We buried the shoe box full of cash under a tupelo tree. Then we shoved off and paddled downriver.

My father used to say that you live most of your life inside your own head, so make sure it's a good space. Easier said than done.

There's no Off switch on my imagination, and I couldn't stop worrying about what the bogus Talbo Chock might be doing to Malley. You see so many awful stories on the news, it's hard not to think the worst. Maybe he was just a harmless, mixed-up guy, or maybe he was a stone criminal. The facts weren't encouraging: He'd stolen a car, sunk it in a river and disappeared with my cousin.

What would I do if I caught him hurting her? All the scenes I imagined had the same violent outcome: I would hurt him worse.

In my whole life I'd never punched anybody, but now I visualized myself going totally psycho, pounding Malley's kidnapper to a bloody pulp. It was pure crazed anger, but that's what boiled up whenever I thought about him laying a hand on her. In reality, of course, it wasn't me that Online Talbo had to fear if we got there before the cops. It was the governor.

After that last phone call, when Malley had made it clear she wanted to get away, I kept wondering why she couldn't. She was tricky—smarter than almost everybody else I knew. Maybe the dude was able to keep her prisoner because he had a gun or a knife. Possibly he'd tied her up, though during our conversation it had sounded like she was walking around.

In my mind I pictured a basic camping situation. All she had to do was wait for a moment when he wasn't paying attention and then take off running. Malley was superfast, and she could go miles without stopping.

Literally *miles*.

But now, as the governor and I canoed down the Choctawhatchee, the problem with my imaginary escape scenario was obvious. On both sides of the river the forest cover was thick, the ground pitted and mucky. Once in a while we'd pass a flat dry clearing or a boat landing, but most of the terrain was dense, tangled and uneven. A person trying to dash through it would be constantly tripping on vines and stumbling over cypress knees. Malley wouldn't have been able to run at half her cross-country speed without twisting an ankle. The chances for a clean getaway would be slim. She'd also have the disadvantage of not knowing which way through the woods led out.

I was kneeling in the front of the canoe; Skink was in

the back. At first I paddled as hard as I could, causing us to slide and zigzag—I couldn't help myself, I was so torqued up about finding my cousin. Canoes obviously can't go as fast as motorboats, and I was worried that Malley's kidnapper was outpacing us.

Skink finally jabbed me with his paddle and told me to save my energy. He said the bogus Talbo was probably looking for a quiet place to lie low along the Choctawhatchee. For a criminal the river was a safer place than the highway, he explained. Fewer people, and way fewer cops.

So I slowed my paddling to match the timing of Skink's stroke. When a big boat went speeding by, we made sure to aim our bow directly into the wake so the canoe wouldn't swamp.

As the sun climbed higher, the breeze quit. Although we kept to the shady side of the river, the air got blistering hot. Whenever we took a break I limited myself to one gulp of water, because we'd brought only four small bottles. The mosquitoes were ridiculous, so the governor located a wax myrtle and snatched two handfuls of leaves as we glided past. We mashed them up and smeared the paste on our arms and necks and faces. After that, the bugs stayed away.

Skink's glass eye fogged up again in the humidity while his good eye scanned the shorelines for any random motion, any sign of life. Every time we approached a bend in the waterway we'd get real quiet, in case Online Talbo and my cousin were around the turn.

The hours passed slowly. Finally we stopped at the mouth of a creek, where Skink took out the fishing rod and tied a spinner-type lure on the line. Right away he caught a nice bass, which he attached to a stringer and trailed behind the canoe.

"Dinner," he said, but I couldn't think about eating. I was prepared to paddle until my arms went numb.

He landed two more fish, and we continued down the river. A little while later he stopped again, though not to cast for bass.

"Look up, Richard. There it is."

"What?" I didn't see anything unusual. "Look where?"

"Hush."

We were drifting past a towering dead cypress that was shaped like the mast of a pirate ship. The tree was leaning slightly, and beards of Spanish moss draped its bone-colored branches.

"That's the tree where I saw the Lord God Bird," Skink whispered. "April 17, 2009."

"Sweet," I said, trying to be polite.

Because, honestly? I didn't believe he'd seen a real live ivorybill. Woodpecker holes were visible up and down the trunk of that old cypress, but probably they'd been drilled by other species. Most likely what the governor had spotted that spring morning had been an ordinary pileated.

Like so many bird watchers, he was guilty of wishful thinking. The ivorybill was extinct, gone forever. Sad but true.

"He was perched up at the very top, right about there." Skink was pointing. "We watched each other for a full minute, then he squeaked three times and flew away."

"Could you see the underwings?"

"Clear as day."

"And the trailing edges were white?"

"What is this, a pop quiz?" he said irritably. "I know damn well what I saw, and what I saw was an ivorybill."

I wasn't going to argue with the man. The only thing that mattered at that moment was Malley. Any other topic was a distraction.

A johnboat came *putt-putt*ing around the bend ahead of us. It had a small outboard engine and one person aboard steering with a tiller. He wore a floppy straw hat and a red bandanna pulled up under the eyes, like a bank robber in the Wild West days.

As the motorboat came closer, the driver gave a small wave.

Skink called out, "How's fishin'?"

The driver turned off the engine and quacked, "What?"

"I said, how's the fishin'?"

"Lousy." It was a woman, not a man. She tugged down the bandanna and lit up a cigarette. I would have guessed her to be in her late fifties, early sixties, and not a fan of dentists.

She pointed behind the canoe, where the bass were swirling on our stringer. "I see you fellas had some luck."

The governor shrugged modestly. "You want one? There's three fish and but two of us."

"Naw. But thanks just the same."

"My name is Clint. This is my grandson, Richard."

"I'm Etta. Pleased to meetcha."

"How you fixed for water, Etta?"

"I'm good." She turned away to blow some smoke.

At this point I started getting pretty annoyed. Not only was Skink wasting precious time socializing with this person, he was trying to give away our food and water.

So I spoke up: "Gramps, we really ought to get going."

He completely ignored me.

"Etta, did you go far downriver?"

"Couple miles is all."

"Reason I ask, we're s'posed to meet up with some folks for supper—Richard's cousin and her new boyfriend. Only we don't know exactly where they're at."

Etta removed her hat. Her hair was cropped short and dyed the color of copper pennies. She scratched a bare spot on her scalp.

"I ran 'crost a young couple down a ways," she said. "Ain't too friendly, though."

"Which side of the river?" the governor asked.

"Same side we on now. They's anchored up in some old houseboat."

"Must be them. How far from here?"

"Not far t'all," she said.

"And they've got the anchor out, you say?"

"That's right. You might could get there by sunset but I wouldn't bet on it."

"Well, we're much obliged."

"Like I mentioned, they ain't real friendly. That young man, he gimme the evil eye when I waved hello. The female, she just sorta stared."

Skink frowned. "There's no excuse for bad manners, is there, Richard?"

"No, sir," I said. Then to Etta: "Sorry about that, ma'am. I'll have a talk with her."

She was eyeing the snake rattle hanging from my neck. "That's one big ol' diamondback."

"Yes, ma'am. Eighteen buttons."

She whistled through one of the many gaps in her teeth. "Whatchu do wit' his skin?"

The governor said the rattlesnake was a roadkill. "The hide got all tore up."

"Too bad." Etta jerked the starter cord and the dinky outboard shook to life. "Say, where'd you catch them fish?"

Skink told her about the good bass creek. She thanked him and continued upriver.

As soon as I took out my cell phone, he asked, "What are you up to, son?"

"Calling Detective Trujillo to tell him where Malley is."

Except I wasn't calling anybody. My battery was dead,

and obviously there was no electrical source on the canoe, no place to plug in a charger. I asked to borrow the governor's cell, which he took from his pants pocket.

The same pants he'd been wearing when he jumped into the river to explore the sunken Toyota.

"You drowned your phone!" I said.

Truly he couldn't have cared less.

I wasn't real happy. "This is bad, dude. I promised my mother I'd call the police as soon as we found Malley."

"We haven't found her yet."

"But if it's her on that houseboat, and neither of us has a phone that works—"

"Well, we could paddle upriver all the way back to the bridge," Skink said, "which would give this jerk more time alone with your cousin. Or . . ."

"Or we go get her ourselves. Is that Plan B?"

"You've always known it was a possibility, Richard. You knew it that night when you got in the car."

He was right. Honestly, I wasn't too surprised that the hunt for Malley was playing out this way, that her rescue would depend on just the two of us—a one-eyed hermit with a mangled foot, and me.

Quite the all-star team.

"Okay, so how do we do this?" I said.

"On a full stomach, when we're not bone-tired." The governor picked up his paddle and stroked toward shore. "It'll be dark in an hour. Let's make camp."

"Right now? But we're so close!"

"They'll still be there in the morning. We need to eat, and we need to rest," he said. "We also need some rules."

"Really? After all this, there's rules?"

"Well, just one."

"Which is?"

"Do whatever I tell you, whenever I tell you. No questions."

"But—"

"Starting now, Richard."

ELEVEN

To say my stepfather isn't an outdoorsman is a kind understatement. If Trent hits a golf ball into the woods, he won't go looking for it because he's basically terrified of nature. Snakes, spiders, ants, lizards, moths, bats, squirrels, opossums—if it doesn't wear shoes, Trent's afraid of it. One time, on the sixteenth fairway of the golf course, the man actually ran from a crow. This I witnessed with my own eyes.

But it's not like he's a total wimp. I remember the afternoon he knocked out a drunk tourist who said something crude to my mother. Trent's a city person, that's all. He grew up in downtown Chicago, a place where there isn't much wildlife except for pigeons. Moving to a small beach town in rural Florida was a huge change, and he's still adjusting. I get that.

His Bigfoot fixation is what made me think of him while the governor and I gathered kindling for a campfire. The thick timber along the Choctawhatchee would be a perfect location for the TV Sasquatch hunters to do an episode of their reality show. One glimpse of Skink, and those goofballs would wet their pants. It would be a You-Tube classic.

When I asked Skink if he'd ever been mistaken for a Bigfoot, he said, "The only thing I get mistaken for is a nut case."

No comment from me.

Soon after we got the flames going, he fell into a deep and sudden sleep. Curled up in the shape of a comma, he didn't look much like a Sasquatch. After the sun went down I felt hungry, but I didn't try to wake him until he started having one of those snarling nightmares. The sounds coming from his throat made the hair on my arms stand up. If Online Talbo was near enough to hear the growls, he'd think there was a rabid panther roaming the forest. Probably haul up the anchor on that houseboat and take off full-speed with Malley.

I was afraid to stand too close, so I used the nine-iron to jostle Skink. Gradually his sounds shrank to soft cries, like a lost kitten would make. I knelt down, spoke his name firmly and shook him by the shoulders. His live eye opened as slowly as a clam.

"It's okay," I said. "You're having another bad dream."

"Are you in it?"

"No. I'm real."

"You sure?"

"Positive. It's me—Richard. Remember?"

He sat up, snatched the front of my shirt and yanked me closer for inspection.

"Well, all right," he said, and let go.

His face and neck were dripping sweat. Hanging from his beard were a pair of june bugs, which he flicked into the shadows.

"Let's make dinner," I suggested.

"Before we move forward, one item of business."

"What?"

"I want to hear your terrible secret," he said. "This hideous crime you say you committed, the one your cousin threatens to blackmail you with."

Out of nowhere! The man goes from barely recognizing me to full-on interrogation mode.

"It's called full disclosure," he said.

"But there's lots of *your* secrets I don't know."

"You know the most important one," Skink said. "You know who I am."

"I'm talking about bad stuff."

"You'll feel better after you tell me."

"No, I'm pretty sure I'll feel like crap."

"Listen up. You need to clear your head before we make our big hero move tomorrow."

"My head *is* clear. Totally." Talking about Saint Augustine was the last thing I wanted to do. "Let me go take those fish off the stringer," I said.

He grabbed my ankle. "You will not."

The strength of his grip was unbelievable. I mean, for an old dude? He could have snapped my lower leg like a chopstick, if he'd wanted to. That's no lie.

"Tell me the heaviest thing you've ever done in your life," I said, "and I'll tell you what I did."

"Deal."

"You go first."

"All right, Richard." He released my ankle. Using the nine-iron, he levered himself to his feet.

"You ready?" he asked.

"Anytime."

But I was so *not* ready. My jaw hung open while Skink told his story. The craziest rumors about him on Wikipedia didn't come close to what he told me that night. I'd write it in these pages, except I promised him I'd never tell a soul.

And I owe the man, big-time. Always will.

"A life such as mine is a treacherous path. These were bad people, son." That was the sum of his explanation. He wore a calm expression as he poked the blade of the golf club into the campfire, sparking embers.

"Your turn," he said to me.

"Right."

"Enough with the drama. Let's hear what you did."

"I stole something."

"Was it cash money?"

"No way. But I walked into a store and took something I didn't pay for."

The governor grunted. "Shoplifting? This is why you're tormenting yourself?"

"It wasn't like stealing a pack of gum!"

"So what was your big score? Diamonds? A Rolex watch?"

"It was a skateboard," I said. "Just the deck, not the wheels and trucks."

He rubbed his brow. "Basically a piece of plywood."

"Maple. And the price was almost two hundred bucks."

"Why'd you take it?" he asked.

"Because I was being an idiot. Mom wouldn't get it for me, even though she knew I'd pay her back."

At the time, I was working three afternoons a week for a guy who owned a mobile car-washing service. He stayed busy on the lower beach road. Some tourists get weird about having salty air touch the paint on their cars, and they're happy to fork out twenty-five dollars for a wash job. My cut was eight bucks, nine for SUVs, plus tips.

"Son, why'd you want that particular skateboard so badly?"

"Because it was exactly like one my father had."

"The one he was riding the day he died."

"Yup," I said.

"An awfully painful reminder for your mother."

"I guess."

Skink was right. That's why she wouldn't buy the board for me—seeing it made her sad.

"Malley was with me that day in the surf shop. She pretended like she was choking to death on a Jolly Rancher, and the guys who work there all ran over to help. I picked up the board and walked out. Nobody noticed."

My cousin had come along with us on the trip to Saint Augustine, where we were meeting my brothers. She let me put the stolen deck in her beach bag so Mom wouldn't see it on the ride home.

As I recounted the story, I was biting through my lower lip. Didn't feel a thing. I told the governor the skateboard was still in my bedroom, hidden in a place my mother would never think to look.

"Let me guess," he said. "It's in the box springs of your bed."

"How'd you know!"

"I was your age once, back when dinosaurs roamed the earth."

"After a couple weeks I had enough money to pay back the shop, but I never did. Guess I was too ashamed. See, the owner was friends with Dad—he came to the funeral and everything."

"He probably would've given you the board for free."

"Yeah." I was an idiot, like I said.

It's a vintage Birdhouse board with sweet Rasta graphics. They don't make that model anymore, and even online they're hard to find. The one my father was riding when he crashed into the UPS truck got run over and split to pieces by the ambulance. I salvaged the wheels and trucks, which I later attached to the deck that I'd lifted from the shop.

"You ever ride it?" Skink asked.

"Never once."

"Understandable."

"So . . . now you know." I expected him to shrug off the whole thing and say that what I'd done was no big deal, crime-wise, but that wasn't his reaction.

"Next time you're in Saint Augustine, do what's right," he said. "Go back to that store and pay the gentleman for his merchandise. This isn't just a piece of grandfatherly advice, Richard. It's a moral instruction."

"Okay, I promise."

"Guilt is a bear. You'll feel liberated afterwards," he assured me. "Now, let's eat while we've still got a fire to cook on. Go fetch the bass."

A soft drizzle had begun, and a storm was rumbling toward us from the south, off the Gulf. I hurried down to the river where we'd beached the canoe, only to find that the canoe had moved.

Was still moving, actually—away from shore, nosing steadily downstream. An empty vessel departing on a straight course, as if steered by a ghost.

Which I didn't believe in. Still don't.

The most likely explanation was a tricky gust of wind or a rogue current. After pulling off my sneakers and emptying my pockets, I was ready to jump in after the runaway canoe.

That's when Skink appeared at my side. All he said was "My fault, son."

Well, that and a curse word.

Bottom line: Don't leave a stringer of fish dangling

too long in a river, especially if the river hosts a hungry population of alligators. The one that was swimming off with our dinner—and towing our canoe—briefly revealed itself with a boiling swish of its thick armored tail.

Definitely not a lazy golf-course gator. Immediately I scrapped my plan to dive into the water.

Watching the canoe disappear around the bend made me feel useless and totally frustrated. It was the worst kind of luck at the worst possible time. If the alligator made a fast dive with the bass in its jaws, either the stringer would snap or the canoe would flip—possibly both.

"What do we do now?" I said gloomily. "How will we reach Malley?"

"I got this." He brushed past me. "Stay here and mind the camp."

Leg splint and all, he hobbled straight into the Choctawhatchee.

"Are you insane? That's a major gator out there!" I yelled.

"'Nature never deceives us. It is always we who deceive ourselves.'"

"What in the world are you talking about?"

"It's from a novel by Rousseau," Skink called back, neck-deep in the flow. "He was the son of a Swiss watchmaker, swear to God. You should goggle him on your computer!"

"It's 'Google.' Now, get out of the water before you get

bit!" I seriously doubted that Rousseau, whoever he was, had been writing about carnivorous river reptiles.

"I'll be returning shortly," the governor declared, and with a splash he went under. A series of fat bubbles appeared, trailing down the current.

Any moment I expected his hairy deep-lined face to pop up for air among the raindrops, but it didn't. A jagged spear of lightning sliced the darkness, and in that ultraviolet moment I could see how completely alone I was.

The wind began swirling as the rain fell harder. Our small fire smoldered and hissed.

I put on my shoes. Wrapped a sleeping bag around my body, trying to stay dry. On the ground lay the governor's lame shower cap, which looked like something my eighty-six-year-old great-aunt would wear. I picked it up and fitted it on my head.

The downpour went on for a long, depressing time. I wasn't hungry anymore.

Thunder shivered the treetops. Our camp turned to puddles and red muck.

I waited and waited. Never once shut my eyes, all night. At daybreak there was still no Skink, and still no canoe.

Just me and the dark river, rising.

TWELVE

I didn't want to give up on the man, but the awful reality of the situation was as clear as a ticking clock.

For a distraction I took out the Rachel Carson book he'd loaned me. At first I wasn't really into it, but then I got to a frightening account of what happened in certain towns when powerful chemicals were sprayed to kill insects like bark beetles and fire ants. Right away the wildlife began dying—squirrels, opossums, rabbits, even the neighborhood cats. Children would awake to dead-silent mornings because all the songbirds had been killed by the poison. Hawks, owls and bald eagles fell sick, too—and those that survived stopped having babies.

All this went down a few years before my mom and dad were born, in the middle of ordinary America. Terrible but true.

Growing up by the ocean, I've always taken birds for granted. How bad would it suck to grow up in a place where life was gone from the skies and the trees? I closed the book and took note of what was visible in the woods—warblers, sparrows, mockingbirds, a lone crow, redwing blackbirds, a pair of cardinals. From the water's edge I could hear king-fishers and ospreys and a croaky blue heron. Somewhere else a northern flicker was hammering on a cypress trunk, which made me wonder how one wood-pecking species managed to survive mankind's dumbass mistakes while others—like the poor ivorybill—didn't make it.

I closed the book, thinking about my own survival issues. Skink would have been back by now, if he were coming. Either the gator had nailed him or he'd drowned from exhaustion while pursuing the loose canoe. It was time for me to face facts—the man was old, half-crippled, and the swollen river was strong. The thought of him dying made me feel empty and sick-hearted, but I couldn't hang around waiting any longer.

He was gone. I was alone.

And Malley was still out there, in trouble.

The idea that I could save her all by myself was crazy, yet I had no choice but to try. There wasn't time to find help—I didn't know which way to run, and it might have taken a day or longer to get out of those woods.

So the only real option was the most reckless and dangerous one. Even though the odds were ridiculous, I didn't let myself think about failing. What I made myself think about was getting it done, period.

Like I can just clap my hands and turn myself into a Navy SEAL, right?

For breakfast: A peanut-butter granola bar and a slug of water from my only bottle. The others had departed on the canoe, along with Skink's fishing rod, a fry pan, a hatchet and other gear that would have been very useful.

Sneaking through the woods, I tried to keep close enough to the river's edge so I could spot the houseboat where Online Talbo was holding Malley. Unfortunately, the water had risen so high that in some places I had to hike inland to stay on dry land.

Which wasn't *that* dry, thanks to the overnight deluge. Several times I sunk up to my ankles in muck. The tread on my sneakers kept slipping on mossy old tree roots—it was a miracle I didn't fall and break my butt. For balance I used the governor's nine-iron, which I figured would also be good for self-defense. It felt heavier than the aluminum ball bat that my mother made me carry on turtle walks.

I tried to creep silently, but the ninja thing wasn't working. When I wasn't sloshing or stumbling, even the softest step forward snapped a few twigs. Since there was no trail for me to follow, I had to make my own.

A cherry-red bass boat went speeding up the Choctawhatchee, its wake knocking sleepy turtles off their logs. The fishermen aboard couldn't hear my shouts over the engine noise and never turned in my direction. They probably had a cell phone, but I never got a chance to borrow it. The boat disappeared from view within seconds.

Although the bugs were vicious, the bottle of repellant stayed zipped inside my backpack. After reading those sickening stories in *Silent Spring*, I felt guilty about squirting chemicals at any living thing, even a mosquito that was guzzling my blood.

As the sun rose higher, the woods heated up and the air got sticky. There wasn't a wisp of a breeze. I stopped to take another sip of water. Okay, two sips. Through the pines I could see I'd made it past that bend in the river, yet no houseboat was in sight. No canoe, either.

What I didn't want to see was a dead body floating—the governor's body—but I braced for that sad sight. By noon I was totally whipped from the tough hike. My legs were sore, my face was splotched with insect bites and I'd torn a hole in the knee of my pants. It got so hot that I finally set my backpack on a cypress knee and waded waist-deep in the water, which felt awesome.

I could've stood there for hours, the cool current streaming around my legs, but another boat appeared, heading upriver. I kept yelling to the driver until he finally saw me, and he made a wide turn toward shore. His boat was slow and low-riding, about twenty feet long with a squared-off bow. A small barge, really. It was piled with dead gars, which was weird because they aren't any good to eat. They're ugly fish, tough-skinned and tubular, with a flat beak of a mouth packed with needle-sharp teeth.

"Whassup?" the man said when he got close.

"Sir, you have a phone?"

"Do not."

The man was unshaven and wore no shirt. Not to be mean, but he could have used a bra. His balding scalp looked sunburned, his chubby face flushed from heat and hard labor. He wore black wraparound sunglasses with the NASCAR logo on the frames.

The boat stunk from the load of gars. I didn't see any gig poles, but the fish definitely had holes in them. Dried blood streaked the man's meaty arms, and slime-green gar scales stuck to the hair on his chest. A swarm of bottle flies was orbiting his melon-sized head.

"Did you pass anybody on your way up the river?" I asked.

The gar gigger just shrugged. Not the friendliest dude. I explained that I was looking for my cousin.

"Sure you are," he said.

"No, seriously. She's staying on a houseboat with a friend of hers. My canoe got away from me last night, so now I don't have any way of reaching her."

"How the hell do you lose a canoe?"

"It happened during the storm," I said, skipping the details. "My name's Richard. Richard Sloan."

When Mom married Trent she took his last name, McKenna. I kept my father's name, and Trent was totally fine with that.

The gar man didn't volunteer an identity. "Didn't see no canoe, but they's a houseboat not far."

"Can you show me where?" I had like seven bucks left in my pocket, sopping wet, and I offered it to him. "To help pay for the gas," I said.

"O-right."

I stepped aboard carrying my backpack and Skink's nine-iron. I could practically hear Mom's frantic voice in my ear: *Richard, have you lost your mind? The guy might be a serial killer!*

Normally I'd never have set foot on a boat with an unknown character, but this wasn't a normal situation. In my mind, it was life or death. The gar man didn't frighten me, though he didn't look particularly dependable. My plan: One wrong move and I'd brain him with Skink's golf club, then dive overboard.

On deck there was no place to stand except among the dead fish, which were slippery. The gar man whisked the seven dollars from my hand. I was determined to get on his good side because I didn't want to go up against Online Talbo one on one.

"What's your name?" I asked.

"Nickel."

"Nice meeting you, Mr. Nickel."

"Ain't my last name. It's my first."

He had ridiculous B.O. I mean he reeked like a porta-potty. Mix that with the gasoline fumes and fish stink, and it was hard to take a breath aboard that boat without gagging.

"Hold on tight," he said, and banged the throttle forward with a bare knuckle.

"Hey, you're going the wrong way."

"Seven bucks gits you to the other side of the river, no farther. Hike down a ways, you'll see the houseboat anchored up beside some mossy oaks."

"Really? You're just going to drop me off and go?"

"Does this look like a taxicab, boy?"

"No, sir," I muttered.

"These garfish ain't gettin' any fresher."

"Whatever." I was bummed, but I didn't want to argue with the man. I couldn't imagine who would buy a boat full of dead gars, or why. Not even Skink would eat one, and he'd eat just about anything.

When we reached the opposite shore, Nickel slowed the engine and nudged the barge into a grassy cove. "Out you go," he said.

"Wait. How do I know you really saw the houseboat? You might just be telling me that to get my money."

"Whoa, you callin' me a liar?"

That's when I noticed the gun propped behind the console. A .22 rifle, the stock glistening with fish slime. Nickel hadn't gigged all those gars—he'd shot them.

"Sorry," I said quickly. "I believe you."

Insulting a stranger is never a brilliant idea, especially a stranger with a gun. Fortunately, the gar man seemed to accept my apology.

"It's maybe twenty-four foot, the houseboat. White with blue trim, but she's all faded out. They's an old Evinrude on the back, a one-fifteen. I didn't see nobody on board when I went by, but they was clothes hung to dry."

"Girls' clothes?" I asked.

"Yeah, some." Nickel seemed embarrassed to have noticed. "Saw a bathing suit."

"Was it yellow?"

"Think so."

A few days before she'd run away, Malley had bought a canary-yellow swimsuit at a surf shop. I felt good about what the gar man was saying because it meant that the houseboat wasn't moving, and that normal things, such as laundry, were getting done.

After thanking Nickel, I stepped gingerly through the fish corpses and hopped from the bow of the barge to the bank.

Shooing the flies from his face, he asked, "You got a gun in your bag, boy?"

"No, sir."

"Huh."

"Dumb question—do I *need* a gun?" I hadn't told the gar man about Malley's situation.

"You'll wish you had one if'n them wild pigs git after you."

Oh great, I thought. Some vicious new beast to worry about.

"The boars is the meanest ones. They tusks'll rip your guts out," Nickel said. "How 'bout you gimme a shove off?"

"Hey, I have an idea."

"Naw, just shove me off."

"If had more than seven dollars to pay, would you consider giving me a ride downriver?" The thought had just popped into my brain. At the slow pace I'd been hiking, the houseboat carrying my cousin might be long gone by the time I got there.

Also, I wasn't thrilled at the idea of being gored by a crazed pig.

"You got more cash?" Nickel asked with a twitch.

"Way more. But not on me."

"Think I'm stupid?"

"Up by the Road 20 bridge?"

"Go on."

"There's a shoe box buried in a secret spot," I said.

It wasn't mine to give away, but the governor was gone and time was running out for Malley. I couldn't think of a better way to keep Nickel interested.

"What kinda secret spot?" he asked.

"I'll tell you where if you give me a ride to the houseboat."

Skink never told me how much money was left, and I hadn't asked. However, when he had opened the shoe box to get the cash for the canoe, I'd seen several thick stacks of bills bundled with rubber bands.

"There's plenty in there," I informed Nickel. "Take what you think is fair."

I figured he'd keep it all. Assume the worst—that was Skink's philosophy.

"You rob a bank, boy, or what?"

"The money belonged to my grandfather. He was an honest man. Once I'm on the houseboat, I'll tell you exactly where to go dig."

The gar man spat over the side. "I don't like being made the fool. They's no shoe box in the ground up there, you gonna see me again real soon. Too soon."

"Dude, I'm telling the truth."

"O-right," he said. "Git back in the boat."

Being heavy, the barge couldn't go very fast, but I didn't mind. It beat slogging on foot through the marsh and the vines.

"M'self, I got sixteen known cousins," the gar man was saying, "and I wouldn't give a dollar fifty for all of 'em put together."

"I only have one cousin. She's like my best friend."

"Yeah, still." He was eyeing me from behind his NAS-CAR shades. "You ain't givin' me the whole story."

"I don't know the whole story, but I'm pretty sure she's in trouble."

Nickel pushed the throttle wide open. The engine sounded dreadful, like marbles in a washing machine. I was afraid it might blow up.

The gar man raised his voice. "This old whale won't do more'n ten knots!"

Good enough, I thought.

He was keeping to the middle of the river. The stench followed us, and so did the bottle flies. Ahead was another bend.

And beyond that bend was a white houseboat with blue trim.

THIRTEEN

A radio was playing. Country-western, which was not Malley's favorite.

Nobody was visible on deck. As we drew closer I called her name. From the corner of my eye I saw the gar man pick up his rifle.

The houseboat was battered and grimy, the paint bleached flat by the sun. Once upon a time the boat had had a name, but the lettering on the transom had faded. The hull looked nicked and gouged. Bolted to the stern was a big outboard engine that was probably older than me. Part of the Evinrude decal had peeled off so that only the "rude" was left.

Laid out on the side rails were my cousin's yellow swimsuit, some T-shirts, four white socks, a men's pair of blue jeans and the gray hoodie that Malley had been wearing the night her mother dropped her at the Orlando airport. I remembered the hoodie from the security video that Detective Trujillo had showed me.

The houseboat's windows were open, but they'd been covered from the inside with bedsheets. Maybe the sheets were meant to keep out mosquitoes, or maybe they were put there to prevent anyone from seeing inside.

Nickel eased the garfish barge alongside. He tied off with a greasy-looking rope. Balancing on the gunwale, he jabbed the barrel of his .22 through one of the houseboat's windows and pulled down the sheet. He took a long look inside before announcing: "Ain't nobody home."

In a way, I was relieved. My fear was finding Malley tied up and gagged.

"What kinda trouble you think your cousin's got into?" the gar man asked.

"I'm not sure yet."

My guess was that Online Talbo had taken Malley ashore to find something to eat. It was only a short swim. He'd probably left the music playing to make people think the boat was occupied, so they wouldn't try to sneak on board and swipe anything.

"Those her clothes hung up to dry?" Nickel said.

"Some of them, yeah."

"Then she ain't dead, is my thought. They'll be back."

"I'll wait." Nervously I climbed aboard. It must have been a pitiful sight, me and my nine-iron, because Nickel said, "You sure 'bout this, boy?"

"Definitely." I wasn't going back without Malley, no way. I flicked the eighteen-button rattle hanging from my neck and said, "It's my good-luck charm."

"Didn't help the snake too much, did it?"

Thanks, I thought, *for the vote of confidence.*

"Look, I cain't stay and watch over you."

"No problem," I told him. "We made a deal. You did your part."

"They's a man in Bonifay gonna pay me two hundred bucks for these fish. Maybe two ten. He grinds 'em up to fertilize his watermelon patches, eighty acres total. But he don't like to wait."

He glanced down at his .22, and for a second I thought he might offer it to me. If he had, I would've said no thanks. The only thing I've ever aimed a rifle at was a Dr Pepper can, and it took five tries to put a hole through it. I was target-shooting out near the landfill with Mitch, a friend of mine who's in tenth grade. He's a serious hunter. My brothers and I never owned any guns. Mom and Dad didn't like them.

"The money," said the gar man. He seemed to be in a hurry.

"Just before you reach the bridge, there's a boat ramp."

"I know which one."

"Ten steps from the ramp is an old tupelo tree. That's where my grandfather's shoe box is buried."

"'Preciate it. You take care." Nickel untied the barge and slowly it drifted away from the houseboat. He gave a slight nod before chugging upriver. The flies went with him, but the stink lingered like a fog.

I got out of sight pretty quick. The inside of the cabin was musty and hot. First thing I did was rehang the sheet that Nickel had yanked down. Small holes along one edge aligned with a row of nails that somebody had hammered into the window frame.

In one corner of the cabin was a portable camp stove. In another sat a scuffed gray suitcase that most likely belonged to the fake Talbo Chock. The suitcase was locked, so I let it be. On the floor was a pile of rumpled blankets along with Malley's red travel bag. I found her laptop, which was broken. Worse than broken, actually—it looked like somebody had stomped on it. No wonder my cousin hadn't been sending any emails.

My plan was to hide as soon as I spotted Malley and the bogus Talbo Chock returning through the woods. There was a hatch in the cabin floor that held a spare anchor, a rusty fire extinguisher and some mildew-covered life vests. I crawled inside to make sure there was enough space for me and my backpack—no problem, once I chased off the spiders.

After stowing my stuff, I propped open the lid of the hatch for easy access. Then I took a seat behind the console. Most of the gauges were cracked from old age and weather. Leaning against a cockeyed compass was a portable clock radio that was playing a song about hard times and lost romance. I wanted to change the channel, but Online Talbo would know something was wrong if he heard rock or hip-hop blasting from the boat.

One thing I didn't factor into my situation was exhaustion. The night before, I hadn't slept for even five minutes. The rain was too noisy, thwopping like BBs against the shower cap. Plus I couldn't stop thinking about the governor, chasing a gator through the dark waters of the Choctawhatchee. Now, in a muggy stillness full of sad guitar tunes, my eyelids grew heavy. I tried cranking up the volume, which rousted me for a while, but eventually I ended up in the middle of a dream that made no sense.

It was me, Trent and my father playing golf on a beach! The two of them were getting along just fine. Mom wasn't there, so it wasn't like she had to make a choice. The sand was whiter than the sand on Loggerhead Beach, and the dunes were taller. We had to be careful where we hit our shots because there were fresh turtle nests everywhere, and from each mound poked a single striped soda straw. Trent snap-hooked a five-iron into the surf, and all three of us waded in to search for his ball. My toes brushed against something hard and smooth, but when I dove underwater I saw that the object was way bigger than a golf ball—it was a sunken car, a white Toyota Camry, with a pellet-sized hole in the rear window. I yelled for my father to come see, but nothing came out of my mouth except bubbles.

I woke up with my forehead resting on the steering wheel of the houseboat. Some people were talking, and they weren't part of the dream. Peeking out the cabin door, I saw only birds and butterflies in the trees along the bank. I crept to a window and moved the sheet slightly, so that I was able to look downriver.

Two figures were approaching in a small boat. At first

I thought it was a kayak, but as they drew closer, I saw it was a canoe.

The canoe.

The one that the gator had carried off. There was no doubt in my mind.

Malley sat in the bow. Phony Talbo was paddling in the back. I recognized his blue Rays cap and mirrored Oakleys from the airport video. He didn't look like a huge guy, though I couldn't be sure from a distance. Malley was in a typical Malley slouch. She was wearing some floppy Australian-type bush hat and pink bracelets on each wrist—not her usual style, but I was totally amped just to see her alive, out in the open.

Yet what about the canoe? The sight of it hardened my sad suspicion that Skink was dead. If he wasn't, he would be the one with Malley, and Online Talbo would be the one in the river.

Whatever conversation my cousin and her kidnapper had been having ended abruptly. In silence they were coming straight toward the houseboat. I grabbed the nine-iron and lay down in the hatch. When I lowered the heavy cover, my arms were basically pinned to my body.

The hatch wasn't much wider than a coffin. The darkness and stale heat were smothering. Every breath I took sounded like the huff of a locomotive. Every heartbeat was like a thunderclap. The air was an acrid mix of mold and gas fumes. I've never been claustrophobic, but I knew I couldn't stay there. One of the anchor prongs was digging into my butt, and the nozzle from the fire extinguisher was poking me in the neck. Some sort of insect, possibly a cockroach, casually crawled across my eyebrows, but I couldn't even reach up to brush it away.

In a panic I kneed open the hatch cover, scrambled out and ducked into the boat's head—basically a small closet built around a mini-toilet. It didn't smell like a spring garden, but I sat down and shut the door. It wouldn't lock because the latch had been pried off.

There was a sharp clack when the aluminum canoe nosed against the houseboat, followed by muted thumps as my cousin and Online Talbo stepped aboard. The two of them entered the cabin, the deck squeaking as they walked. Somebody turned off the radio.

"Light the stove." It was a male voice.

"I'm not hungry."

"You're never hungry."

"I won't eat a catfish," Malley said. "They're so gross."

"Gimme your hand."

"No."

"Give it here."

"No!"

I heard a brief scuffle and then a click.

"You're such an ass," Malley snapped.

The fake Talbo called her the b-word. "I'll go clean the fish," he said, "but first I gotta take a whiz."

"Oh nice."

"Don't go anywhere. Ha ha."

Trapped on the toilet, I didn't have any brilliant ideas. The guy needed to relieve himself, and the boat had only one place to do that. I reached for the doorknob and held on. With the other hand I started shaking the rattle on my neck.

A real rattlesnake can vibrate its tail more than fifty times per second, way faster than human finger muscles can move. I must have been trembling like crazy, because the eighteen buttons on that rattle started making some noise—enough to freak out the Talbo impostor.

He let go of the doorknob and yelled, "Whoa! You hear that!"

"What is it?" asked Malley.

"Diamondback!"

"No way. How'd it get on the boat?"

"They can swim, you dummy. Just like moccasins."

"Where are you going? Don't leave me here like this!"

"I'm gonna get that ax from the canoe," Online Talbo declared.

I heard him stomp toward the transom. Rising slightly, I cracked the door just enough so that Malley could see me. Her eyes got wide.

So did mine. Her hair was dyed jet black, even blacker than her jeans. She looked scrawny, and both arms were covered with mosquito bites. The pink bracelets I'd thought I'd seen weren't bracelets at all—they were raw marks made by handcuffs.

One of the cuffs was now locking her by a wrist to the

steering wheel of the houseboat. She opened her mouth to say something, but I signaled her to be quiet. Then I sat down slowly on the mini-toilet and closed the door.

Online Talbo was returning with Skink's hatchet, and I had nothing to defend myself with. The nine-iron was down in the deck hatch, where I'd stupidly left it.

I heard Malley say, "Don't go in there, T.C.!"

"Hey, there's only one way to deal with a damn rattler."

"But what if you get bit?"

"Just shut up. I'm gonna chop that thing into a million pieces!"

I had maybe two seconds to make a decision, and what I decided was this: I didn't particularly want an ax blade embedded in my forehead.

So I hollered, "Stop! I'm *NOT* a snake!"

Silence on the other side of the door, then murmurs of confusion.

Finally, Online Talbo spoke up. "Come outta there right now! Whoever you are!"

I did what I was told. He was poised to strike, holding the hatchet high.

"Chill out, dude!" I raised my hands.

Malley said, "He's just a kid, T.C."

He lowered the hatchet, though he didn't put it down. "Who are you?"

"Carson is my name," I answered.

Malley shot me a look, like: *Where'd you get that one?*

"Carson what?" asked the fake Talbo.

"Just Carson." It probably popped into my head because of Rachel Carson, the author of *Silent Spring*.

"I can't tell you my last name," I said, "because you'll call my parents."

Malley immediately synced to my act. "So you're a runaway!"

"Walkaway is more like it. Let's just say I'm traveling."

"How'd you get out to this boat?" demanded Online Talbo. "You didn't swim, else your clothes'd be wet."

"Hitched a ride with a gar man."

"Bull!"

The bogus Talbo was several inches taller than me—as tall as my brother Robbie only not as muscular. He wasn't ugly and he wasn't movie-star handsome. Regular-looking is what he was, except for his smashed nose, all swollen and plum-colored. That explained the nasal twang.

His dusty brown hair was cut short, and he hadn't shaved in days. His T-shirt was forest green, his jeans were frayed and his white slides were filthy. When he took off his shades I noticed that his dark eyes seemed small and jumpy, like mouse eyes on a rabbit face.

"What was that noise behind the door?" he asked.

I showed him the rattlesnake rattle, which he tore off the cord around my neck and held up in the light. "This the real deal?"

"For sure."

"Too bad." He sneered and threw the rattle out the window, into the water.

"Seriously, dude? That was a present from my grandpa."

"Get offa my boat, dorkface."

While Malley was cyberdating the fake Talbo, she would always brag that he was "deep, like a poet." I'd never met any genuine poets, but I was pretty sure they didn't use the word "dorkface" in everyday conversation.

I turned to my cousin. "How come you're chained to the wheel?"

Bogus Talbo didn't like the question.

Malley smiled tightly and jangled the cuffs. "Oh, it's just a fun game we play sometimes. Right, T.C.?"

"Yeah," he said gruffly.

"Now gimme the key, sweetie."

"What?"

"Come on. Playtime's over," she said. "Carson can help you unload the canoe."

She held out her free hand and wiggled her fingers. "Key?"

Online Talbo was in a jam. He didn't want me to know he was holding Malley against her will. Then he'd be forced to lock me up, too, so that I couldn't go tell anybody.

Still, he wasn't foolish enough to give the key to Malley. He skulked over to the steering console and un-locked her.

"Hey, you can't stay here," he said again to me. The

152

hatchet was in his left hand. He wasn't waving it or anything, but the message was clear.

"I need something to eat, that's all. Then I'll go."

"T.C. caught a big fat catfish," my cousin said.

"I'll help you guys skin it."

"Awesome," said Online Talbo, again with zero enthusiasm.

We walked out of the cabin toward the stern of the boat.

"What's your name?" I asked Malley innocently.

"Louise," she replied with a straight face.

I couldn't stop staring at her tar-black hair. It made her look older, and pale as a witch.

"That's a sweet canoe," I remarked.

"Yeah, we lucked out. It just came floating around the corner this morning."

"Weird. Nobody was in it?"

"Nope."

"Finders, keepers," said the phony Talbo.

His busted nose made me wonder if the canoe really had been empty. Maybe the governor had paddled up to the houseboat and a fight had broken it. Usually I could tell when Malley was holding something back, but it didn't look like she was.

All I wanted to do was whisk her away from the kidnapper, which is what you call somebody who handcuffs a girl—a kidnapper, not a boyfriend. He was already ticked off about me being there, some smartass stowaway interrupting his river cruise, but I didn't mind keeping him off balance. Criminals make mistakes when they feel some heat. That's what Detective Trujillo told me.

Maybe I should have tried a different strategy with the Talbo impostor—like pretending to make friends—but I couldn't force myself to be nice to the man, not even fake nice.

I waited until he'd put the hatchet in his waistband before asking what "T.C." stood for.

"Talbo Chock," he replied smoothly.

I went back right at him. "Dude, I don't think so. No way."

"Whaaaaat?" He was scowling and trying to sound tough, but there was an edge of alarm in his tone.

"The only Talbo Chock I ever heard of is dead," I said.

"Maybe there's more than one. You think a that?"

I shrugged. "More than one guy called *Talbo*? Yeah, whatever."

"Let it go," snapped Malley.

"No problem," I said. "Or as they say down south, no *problemo*."

"I'm not lettin' go of nuthin'," snarled the impostor. "This little turd just called me a liar."

All things considered, I stayed incredibly calm. "Talbo Chock got killed in Afghanistan," I said. "He was in the Marines. They had the service down in Fort Walton Beach and even the mayor was there. No offense, man, but if you're gonna swipe somebody's name, don't pick a war hero."

The kidnapper's face turned purple. "I oughta knock your damn teeth out!"

He took a wild swing, but I ducked.

My cousin stepped between us. "Mind your own business, Carson."

"Sorry, dude," I said to the phony Talbo. "No reason to freak."

But freaked he was.

FOURTEEN

Malley said, "His real name is Tommy Chalmers."

"You shut up!" he bellowed. "Right this minute! Shut up, or else."

"And my name's not Louise. It's Malley."

I couldn't figure out if she wanted me to come clean, too. Honestly, I was fine with staying "Carson" for a while. It was better if Tommy didn't know that Malley and I were related, or that I was the one she'd called with the woodpecker clue.

"I said shut up, both of ya!" His lower jaw was grinding back and forth like a steam shovel.

"God, can you just chillax?" my cousin said. "Carson's cool. Tell him what you told me, okay? He'll understand totally."

Tommy took a minute to get the words lined up before saying: "Talbo was a superclose friend of mine!" Another lie. I knew Tommy had gotten Corporal Chock's name from the funeral papers he'd found in the Toyota that he stole from the preacher.

"When he died," Tommy went on, "it's like I got hit by a Mack truck. His folks called me down in Orlando to gimme the news, and it was like a part of me croaked, too. Know what I'm sayin'?"

"So then he started calling himself Talbo," Malley said. "Right, T.C.?"

"Yeah. Hearing people say his name, that made me feel better. Like, in a way he was still alive."

One of the lamest b.s. stories ever. Still, I said, "Sure. I get that."

"I didn't mean no disrespect. I loved the man."

"Worshipped him," added Malley. "This is T.C.'s grieving process."

I couldn't believe she spoke those words with a straight face. That's when I realized what she was trying to do—calm Tommy down by acting like she was on his side. Her eyes told the cold truth. I was dying to find out what exactly he'd done to her, but that part would have to wait until she and I were alone.

"Come on, let's eat," she said.

Tommy Chalmers snorted. "Thought you weren't hungry."

"Well, *I'm* starved," I said.

The catfish was lying in the bottom of the canoe near Skink's spinning rod. There was no sign of the stringer that had held our bass. Tommy unloaded a six-pack of beer, a small cooler of ice and a five-gallon gasoline container, the same type I carry on my boat back home. Where he'd gotten the gas and ice I didn't know, but it couldn't have been too far from the river.

I offered to skin and gut the fish, but Tommy said, "Just stay outta my way."

When he wasn't looking, Malley stuck out her tongue at him. I mouthed the words, "What happened to his nose?"

She raised her right hand clenched into a fist. I felt another hot rush of anger toward Tommy. Maybe my cousin had punched him for smashing her laptop, or maybe he'd done something worse.

I considered making a hero move for the nine-iron, but then what? The truth: When it came to fighting, I had no self-confidence and zero experience. Dad was opposed to violence of any sort, and it's one of the few things he was superstrict about. My brothers got grounded every time they smacked each other, and they knew better than to ever smack me, the smallest one in the family. Consequently, I had no idea how hard a punch I could take. What I did know was that Tommy Chalmers outweighed me by at least fifty pounds. An ambush seemed like the best chance I had.

The next question was whether or not I could hit any man, even a lowlife criminal, while his back was turned. The answer turned out to be no. The rage I'd felt, those brave fantasies about pummeling my cousin's kidnapper— all of it stayed locked inside. I didn't do a darn thing except stand there like a worthless wimp, watching the Talbo impersonator try to kill our lunch in the bottom of the canoe.

Besides *The Bigfoot Diaries* and cage fights, my stepfather's third-favorite TV show is the one where overweight rednecks jump into muddy rivers to wrestle ginormous catfish. It's pretty sick, and those guys definitely know what they're doing. Catfish can live a while out of water, as Tommy was finding out. They also have fin spines that are covered with toxic slime, and you do *not* want to get stabbed. A fishing guide in Loggerhead Beach told me it's the worst pain ever, then comes the infection. His foot had swelled up like a roasted chicken.

Strange as it seems, the bigger catfish are actually the easiest to handle. Smaller ones are more slippery, and their spines are sharper. Tommy's prize weighed only about three pounds, but even if I'd warned him to be careful, he was too macho to pay attention.

"I know what I'm doin'," he proclaimed to Malley.

Wrong.

His scream was epic. On and on it went. Bone-chilling, as they say. On both sides of the river, spooked birds shot out of the treetops.

My cousin covered her eyes. The dorsal spine of the catfish had gored the palm of Tommy's right hand and was poking through the other side like a knitting needle. He was basically impaled.

At that instant I should have shoved the creep out of

the canoe and paddled away with Malley. That's what the old governor would have done.

Me? I almost fainted. Pathetic but true.

Dark red streams ran down Tommy's right arm while the catfish dangled there writhing. It was a visual I'd like to forget but probably never will. My head got foggy and my knees started to buckle, so I grabbed for the rail of the houseboat.

Peeking through her fingers, Malley noticed my wobbly condition and hissed, "Don't you dare faint!"

By now Tommy's dungeon scream had dissolved into poodle-style yelps. That didn't bother me as much as the blood spouting from his punctured hand. The wound looked a hundred times worse than the gash that the turtle-egg thief had put in Skink's scalp.

"I can't pull it off!" Tommy roared. "I'm stuck!"

"Just cut it, dude," I said weakly.

His unpunctured hand located the hatchet in his belt. Feverishly he began whacking at the catfish. I totally expected to see human fingers scattered like carrot sticks in the canoe, but Tommy's aim was surprisingly good. With repeated sharp chops he managed to sever the spike at the base of the fin. Howling, he yanked it from his flesh. The injured catfish went sailing overboard and, amazingly, swam away.

Lunch was stale potato chips.

* * *

Mom says life is about making the most of your opportunities. I'd wasted a huge one. Tommy Chalmers had been an easy target—doubled over with pain, totally distracted. One good push and he's in the river.

But, no, I'm too freaking dizzy to move. Unbelievable.

Now all three of us were back inside the houseboat's cabin because it was blazing hot out on the deck, and a bold new herd of flies was buzzing around the bloody canoe. Tommy had wrapped his holey hand in a dirty Imagine Dragons T-shirt.

He drank a beer, while Malley and I shared a lukewarm bottle of water. When another bass boat sped past, he ordered both of us to sit tight. It was depressing to see him feeling better.

"So, Carson, where you from?" he asked.

"Pensacola." As good a place as any, I thought.

"Why'd you run away from home?"

"Got in trouble," I said.

"Yeah? Like for what?"

"Stealing a yacht." It sounded more impressive than stealing a car. As long as I was inventing a new life history, why not go full-on outlaw?

Tommy sniggered. "You didn't steal no yacht."

"Hundred-and-twenty-footer. They caught me halfway to Havana. There was a story in the Tampa papers, you don't believe me."

A total bluff.

"So you're a pirate," said Tommy sarcastically. "Like Blackbeard 'cept you can't even grow one."

Malley's eyes were flashing. "Did they put you in jail?"

"Juvie hall," I said. "My folks bailed me out, right? But I didn't want to stick around for a trial. The judge knew me from other times. He was not a fan."

Tommy wasn't buying any of it. Or if he was, he didn't want Malley to think he was.

"So, what was this so-called yacht you stole?" he asked.

"It's called *Lola's Chariot*." Where that name came from is a mystery. I've never met anybody named Lola.

"I'm gonna Google it," Tommy said, "soon as we get to somewhere I can charge my laptop."

Malley told him to stop hogging the chips. "I want to hear more about Carson," she said.

"Well, I don't." Tommy jerked the thumb of his good hand toward the cabin door. "Time for you to go, Captain No-Beard."

"Make you a deal," I said. "I'll go catch us some nice bass if you let me hang around for dinner."

"Ha! I can catch all I want anytime." He wanted me to believe he was an ace survivalist, but the confidence in his voice wasn't real. After the catfish fiasco he wasn't keen on trying again.

"I'll let you cast," he said, "but I'm ridin' along in the canoe."

I was hoping he'd say that. My scheme was to head upriver and trick him into stepping ashore. Then I'd leave him there, paddle like crazy back to the houseboat and pick up Malley.

"Hey, I wanna come, too," she said.

Tommy told her the canoe wasn't big enough.

"He's right," I chimed in.

Malley speared me with her famous ice-princess stare. She didn't want to be left behind—or maybe she didn't want me to be alone on the water with Tommy Chalmers. Just because she didn't act afraid of him didn't mean she wasn't. My cousin likes to give the impression that she's always in control, unfazed by anything or anybody.

"Wait outside," Tommy said, and closed the cabin door behind him.

I searched the canoe for the hatchet. It wasn't there. Under the backseat I spotted the shiny spinner that Skink had used to fool those three bass. I tied the lure to the clear mono line on the fishing rod using an improved clinch knot, which my brothers had taught me when I was little.

Malley and Tommy were still talking inside. I couldn't make out the words, but the conversation didn't sound warm and friendly.

I began casting and reeling in, making a clockwise sweep of the open water behind the houseboat. To test my aim, I threw the lure at brush piles and half-submerged logs, the sort of places where fish like to lurk. I wanted Tommy to see that I knew how to handle a spinning rod.

When he finally emerged, the small ax was again wedged in his belt—definitely not part of my clever plan.

It dawned on me that possibly he didn't care if I caught any fish for dinner; the canoe ride offered him an easy way to get rid of a pesky intruder.

"Let's you and me go," he said.

"Wait, I just had a strike."

"Just now? You're full a crap."

"No, I swear."

I was stalling big-time. The fishing expedition had been a truly bad idea, possibly one of my worst. Tommy Chalmers wasn't dumb enough to let me scam him. He planned to either abandon me somewhere along the Choctawhatchee or chop me into little pieces, as he'd threatened to do to the imaginary rattlesnake in the toilet.

I reeled in fast and made another long cast to the same imaginary fish in the same imaginary spot.

"You deaf? I said let's go!" The canoe rocked when Tommy stepped in.

"There he is!" I yelled, giving the rod a hard jerk.

"Just sit down and shut up."

"No, but look!"

I don't pray often (and I definitely wasn't praying when it happened), but what else could it have been except an honest-to-God miracle? Out of the river rocketed a big bronze-shouldered bass, and hooked in its bucket mouth was the silvery spinner attached to my line.

Twice more the bass jumped as Tommy watched dumb-struck, clutching his bloody wrapped hand. One thing I know how to do is fight a fish, and I whipped that sucker in no time flat. A five-pounder, and that's no bull.

"Enough for all of us," I said, all casual, hoisting the bass by its lower lip.

At first Tommy was quiet. By his clouded expression you could tell that his brain was sorting through the options. Part of it apparently was reminding him how hungry he was.

"Don't drop that thing over the side!" he barked.

"Hey, Malley, come look at this," I called out.

"Never mind her. She's busy." Tommy hopped from the canoe to the deck of the houseboat.

I unhooked the bass, a gleaming wet slab of muscle. Releasing it back in the river would have felt good, but I needed a solid meal. If I was headed for a fight with Tommy, I'd have no chance of winning on an empty stomach.

"Malley, come here!" I shouted once more as I carried the fish aboard.

Her voice from the cabin: "Uh, I can't."

"Why not?"

"I said never mind about her," Tommy barked. "I'll get a knife."

When he opened the door, I saw why Malley couldn't come out. Tommy had handcuffed her to the steering wheel again.

"It's just a game," he said, "like she told you before."

"What kind of stupid game—"

"Nice fish, Carson!" Malley found a way to smile, don't ask me how. Plainly she was miserable.

Tommy insisted on cutting up the fish himself, pinning it to the deck with his bandaged paw. I could have done a better job, twice as fast, but I guess he didn't want to put the knife in my hands.

Probably a smart idea.

FIFTEEN

Tommy said it was too hot to cook, so for a couple hours we sat around the cabin doing nothing. Talk about awkward. He didn't say three words. Obviously, he didn't want to leave me and my cousin alone. Even when he went to the bathroom, he left the door cracked, so he could keep an eye on us.

Finally, when it started getting dark, he lit the portable stove and stepped outside for a smoke.

"Are you okay?" I whispered to Malley.

"He's a whack job, Richard. Totally nuts. He won't let me go!"

"Has he . . . hurt you?"

"Not as much as I hurt him." She re-enacted her punch to Tommy's face. "First he drowned my phone and later he busted my laptop, 'cause he didn't want me emailing. And check out my hair!"

"Shhhh," I said.

"He made me dye it this color after we saw one of those hideous Amber Alert billboards. Did Mom give them that loser picture of me with my braces? She knows how much

I hate that one! Now the whole state of Florida thinks I look like a gopher."

Classic Malley.

"Not so loud," I warned her.

Through the cabin window I watched Tommy pace the deck, dragging on his cigarette. He was shaking his wounded catfish hand like that would make the pain go away. This sounds pretty dark, but I was hoping he'd get a supernasty infection and his whole arm would turn green and fall off. That's how angry I was, deep at the core.

"The canoe," I said to Malley, "tell the truth. Was there anyone in it? Like a tall one-eyed dude with a beard?"

"Seriously?"

"He's a friend of mine. He brought me here to find you."

My cousin swore that the canoe had been empty when they'd spotted it.

"Then he must be dead," I murmured, more to myself than to Malley.

"What? Don't say that about anybody, Richard."

The cabin door swung open and Tommy swaggered in, stinking like an ashtray. "Time to eat," he said, uncuffing my cousin.

We coated the bass filets in cornmeal and pan-fried them—possibly the best meal ever, but then I was hungrier than I could ever remember. Tommy used a real fork but he gave us plastic ones, which were worthless as weapons. We were outside on the rear deck of the houseboat, Tommy scanning the river in case another boat ventured too close. He was on his third beer, but he didn't look sluggish enough for me.

I was studying him closely. A variety of superheroic scenarios sprang into my head, but none of them would work as long as the man stayed wide awake.

During dinner Malley didn't say much. She was wearing that Australian bush hat pulled down low, and she wouldn't look up from her food. I felt bad for her. Getting chained up like a prisoner had to be humiliating.

Meanwhile the meal of fried bass had made Tommy more talkative. I was curious to hear what kind of lie he'd make up, so I asked him how his nose got hurt.

"Ha! You should see the other dude." He gave a stage laugh. "Maybe when they let him out of the hospital, right?"

"What was the fight over?"

"God, I don't even remember."

"I do," said Malley.

"No, you don't." Tommy's voice turned hard. It was a warning to my cousin to keep quiet about what had really happened.

She sighed sarcastically and shook her head. Tommy glared. I steered the conversation elsewhere.

"So what do you do?" I asked him.

"You mean, like, for work?"

No, jackass, I thought, *like, for kite surfing*.

"I'm a DJ," he said. "I do, you know, private events. Clubs sometimes."

"Around here?" I was pretty sure that Walton County wasn't famous for its rave scene.

"I've had major gigs in Orlando, Tampa, South Beach," said Tommy. "Summer slows down, so I'm taking a break."

"What kind of music?" I asked.

Tommy shrugged. "Hip-hop. Dubstep. House. Whatever they want, I play."

"How about country? I heard a country station on the radio when I got here."

"Ain't no freelance DJs on the country scene. The music's all right, but, like, there's no party work."

"Is this your houseboat?"

"Guy I know loaned it to me."

I played along like I believed him. The houseboat was likely stolen, same as the car.

Malley spoke up. "T.C. also writes poetry."

"No way."

"True," said Tommy. "I can rhyme anything. It's a gift, bro."

"Really? Tell me something that rhymes with orange."

He thought about it for a few moments, his lips moving every time he tested a word that might fit. Malley was chuckling under her hat.

Tommy said, "What about mange? Like when a dog gets scabby all over."

"Mange rhymes with arrange," I pointed out, "not orange."

"I bet it all rhymes in French."

"Unbelievable," Malley snorted.

"Hey, French counts!"

Tommy was getting pissed off. Time to change the subject.

"So what's the deal with you guys?" I asked, acting clueless. "Are you two, like, together?"

My cousin said, "We're just friends."

"We're gettin' married," stated Tommy, like it was a done deal.

"Oh, wow. Way to go." I stole a glance at Malley, but I still couldn't see her expression.

Married?

"When's the big day?" I asked.

"Sunday," Tommy told me. "Sunrise on the beach at Destin."

"Cool," I said. "Will the bride be wearing handcuffs?"

"Ha! That's a good one."

"Not funny," said Malley.

Tommy told her to lighten up.

"Doesn't seem like she's into it," I remarked.

"You don't know crap about crap," the poet said.

Here's what I *did* know: My cousin wasn't legally old enough to get married, and she wouldn't have married a stone loser like Tommy at any age, for any reason.

She collected our plates and rinsed them off with river water.

"You got a preacher lined up for the wedding?" I asked.

"Nah, I'm doin' it myself," Tommy said.

"That legal?"

"I wrote the sacred vows for both of us. Right, honey?"

Malley seemed to wince at hearing him say that word. *Honey.* It creeped me out, too.

"Do they rhyme?" I asked. "The vows, I mean."

"You kidding? 'Our hearts were made to be together, in rain or hail or sunny weather. The journey we begin is epic, a love that will forever stay fantastic.'"

"Wow." What else could be said? It was hideous.

My cousin bowed her head and pressed her knuckles to her temples, like she did when she got one of her headaches.

She said, "Know what else rhymes with epic? Ickkk."

Tommy Chalmers turned to me. "Dinner's over. Time for you to go."

"But it's almost dark," Malley objected.

Tommy gave a mean grin. "Pirates ain't scared of the dark, right? Now, go on, Captain No-Beard, get outta here."

What you might call a moment of decision.

"But I like it here," I said. "You guys are cool."

Tommy scratched a mosquito bite on his neck. "You got thirty seconds."

Malley took off her hat. With acid in her voice she asked, "Thirty seconds to do what, T.C.?"

"To jump in the water and swim to shore," the kidnapper said. "Unless the pirate boy don't know how to swim."

"I'll sleep out here on the deck and stay out of your way. Promise."

"Are you deaf," Tommy said to me, "or just dumb?"

"I'm tired is all. Full night's sleep, I'll be good to go."

"Dude, you're going *now*." He rose and took a step in my direction. "Get offa this boat!"

"What if I said no?"

"Then I'd do this."

All of a sudden Tommy was waving a gun—a silver-plated revolver. Don't ask me where it came from. Maybe he'd been hiding it in the back of his jeans.

My cousin said, "Put that thing away."

Meaning she'd seen the pistol before, which explained a few things.

"Just chill out," I said to him. My voice cracked high and brittle.

"Move," he rasped, "or this is gonna be you."

He turned and fired at a tall blue heron that was standing on the riverbank, minding its own business. The bullet pinged off a cypress stump, causing the bird to squawk and flap.

Tommy took aim again. I didn't wait for the shot, though I heard it the instant my skull struck him flush in the ribs. He went down still clutching the pistol, and I was more or less on top of him, Malley screaming at both of us.

Tommy and I got all tangled up, grunting and huffing.

It was a joke, really, me trying to overpower a guy so much bigger.

What was I thinking when I tackled him? I *wasn't* thinking. It was pure reflex, no brainwork whatsoever. The jerk had a loaded gun! Shooting at that bird was bad enough, but now he was one arm twist from shooting *me*.

You always read about people in hairy situations "fighting for their lives," and I definitely can say it's not an exaggeration. My wrestling match with Tommy Chalmers was wildly desperate and awkward—nothing like what you see in the movies. I kept thinking about my mother, how devastated she would be if I never came home.

Somehow I managed to pin the sweaty wrist of Tommy's gun hand until he started slugging me with his free hand, which happened to be the one that the catfish gored. It had swollen up like a melon beneath the bloody T-shirt, and the padding didn't help either of us much. Each blow probably hurt Tommy more than it did me, but he didn't quit until he caught me square in the gut. The air gushed from my lungs and I felt myself deflating like a cheap raft.

With no strain Tommy shook free of my grasp, and at that point I assumed I had only seconds to live—not enough time to tell my cousin how sorry I was for botching the rescue. Not enough time for a single tear.

But then somebody seized me from behind by the shoulders. Suddenly I was hanging in midair, legs kicking, and I remember being totally impressed. I knew Malley was strong, but this was amazing. . . .

Except there she stood, six feet away, staring up at me. Her mouth hung open.

Tommy had squirmed to a sitting position, using his kneecaps to steady the pistol. His eyes were bugging wide, too.

A low voice from above said, "So this is the youth of America."

I wheezed a yell, and twisted around to see his face.

"*Hola, amigo!*" said Skink.

From the looks of him, I figured I was either dreaming or dead.

SIXTEEN

Some images are scorched in your memory, for better or worse. The gator had done an epic job on the old governor.

He was shoeless, shirtless and bareheaded, so the damage was on full display—seeping tooth wounds in his neck, a partial bite imprint on one shoulder, a grid of vivid welts on his chest that matched the armored ridges of the reptile's tail. He had emerged from the river sopping and crowned with slimy hydrilla weeds that made him look like some sort of demented sea monarch. Among the sprigs of his beard dangled moist purplish leeches, several of which had attached to his hide-like cheeks.

Battered and punctured, he still stood ramrod straight like the soldier he'd been half a century ago. During the struggle with the alligator his fake eyeball must have popped out, because the socket was now plugged with a glossy brown snail's shell. His camo pants were blood-splotched, although his smashed foot didn't look as bad as I'd remembered. That was probably because the rest of him looked worse.

Waggling in a corner of the governor's mouth was what

I first thought was a cigarette, except they don't make cigarettes with red stripes. It turned out to be a soda straw just
like the one he'd used for underground breathing on the
beach. This straw had been used for breathing, too, during
his silent, submerged approach to the houseboat.

After lowering me to the deck he said, "That heron
flew away, in case any of you were wondering."

"Who *are* you?" I blurted, figuring it would be best if
Tommy Chalmers didn't know that Skink and I were a
team.

"He's hurt. He needs help," Malley said.

"Nobody move. I mean *nobody*!" Tommy wasn't sure
whom to aim at—the scrawny runaway who'd attacked
him or the cockeyed intruder. He kept jerking the gun
barrel back and forth from me to Skink, who didn't seem
particularly concerned.

"Son, why'd you shoot at that lovely bird?" he asked.
"The only acceptable excuse would be a brain injury. Are
you afflicted in such a way?"

"Shut your trap!" Tommy growled. "Talk about *me*
being mental, what's the deal with putting that bowl in
your eye?"

"It's the shell from an apple snail that no longer
needs it."

"Creepy, period," said my cousin, disappearing into the
cabin.

Calmly, Skink turned and peed over the side of
the houseboat.

"Hey, knock it off!" Tommy protested.

"Overactive bladder," the governor whispered. "You reach my age, the plumbing starts to sputter."

Tommy stood up. "You escape from a homeless shelter, or was it a nut house?"

Skink zipped his trousers. "Son, if you have any redeeming qualities, I advise you to reveal them."

"My name's Carson," I interjected. "This is Tommy."

"Pleased to meet you, *Carson*." Mischief glinted in Skink's live eye. He gave an assuring wink when Tommy glanced away. "You must be mighty fond of birds," he said to me, "to risk taking a bullet for one."

"He's as crazy as you," Tommy fumed.

Malley returned with a first-aid kit. "Here's Band-Aids and some antibiotics. I'd do it myself, but the truth is you really smell."

She could be cold, my cousin.

"I do carry a funk," Skink said agreeably. "It's the raw life I lead. Do you have a name, young lady?" As if he didn't know.

"Malley Spence," she replied. "What happened to you? I mean, you're a disaster—no offense."

"I went after a gator. We fought to a draw."

There was a startling crack of thunder and the Choctawhatchee lit up. With all the turmoil aboard, none of us had noticed the wall of weather rolling in. The wind started howling, and with it came lashes of hard chilly rain.

Tommy angrily ordered us into the cabin, where the governor dressed his alligator wounds and hummed a tune I didn't recognize. Malley sat cross-legged on the floor. scrutinizing the old man with a mix of curiosity and suspicion. As I knelt down beside her, I felt a sharp pain in my ribs where Tommy had punched me.

He stayed on his feet, his back pressed against the cabin door. I noticed he'd switched the pistol to his uninjured hand. "Who are you? What're you doin' out here?" he barked hoarsely at Skink.

"I believe you've found my canoe."

"That's yours?" my cousin asked, though by now she'd realized this unusual character was the bearded accomplice I'd told her about.

"It got away from me upstream," Skink said.

"Too bad" was Tommy's response. "Finder's keepers is the law of the sea."

"But we're not on the sea. We're on a *river*," Malley needled.

"Same deal!"

The governor spit out the straw. "In any case, I'd appreciate the prompt return of my vessel. Please."

It seemed like I was the only one worried about being shot, the only one paying attention to the loaded gun. Skink and Malley were speaking to Tommy as if he were waving a harmless cucumber.

"No way," he said. "That canoe's mine now."

The rain was pelting the boat so loudly that he said it

twice, to make sure he'd been heard. Skink's reaction was to begin picking leeches from his face and popping them into his mouth like junior Twizzlers.

Malley groaned. "That is so incredibly gross."

Skink shrugged. "Nourishment, child."

He sure knew how to make a first impression.

"Stop right now!" Tommy shouted over another boom of thunder.

The governor wiped a sleeve across his blood-flecked lips. "Since you refuse to give back my canoe, I'll be quietly on my way."

"Me, too," I piped, knowing that he wasn't going far, that soon he'd be hatching a new scheme to save Malley. "Dude, thanks for letting me hang for dinner," I said to Tommy, as if we hadn't been fighting ferociously only minutes earlier.

He stomped one shoe and declared that nobody was going anywhere until he said so.

"Don't move." His plugged little rat eyes flicked around the cabin. He looked edgy and stressed. Overwhelmed, really.

Malley said, "What's your problem, T.C.? If these two are dumb enough to swim through a lightning storm, let 'em go."

"No, no, I gotta think."

The governor said thinking was highly overrated, which made me and my cousin laugh in spite of the situation. At that point Tommy's sense of humor was basically nonexistent. After our tussle on the deck, I'm sure he believed that his revolver was the only thing between him and a mutiny.

He made Skink and me sit side by side with our legs extended, then tried to handcuff us together. The cuffs wouldn't fit around either of the governor's thick wrists, which really annoyed Tommy. He told Malley to get the rope off the spare anchor, and pointed to the hatch where I'd stashed my backpack and the nine-iron. She opened the lid and started kicking stuff around, griping the whole time.

Tommy's face beaded with sweat, and he grinded his jaws to fight off the pain from his catfish injury. It appeared to me he was getting sick, which was bad news for him but good news for the rest of us.

After Malley found the rope, Tommy instructed her how to tie us up, since he was unable to do it himself. With him hovering at her shoulder, she bound my wrists behind me and did the same to Skink using double half hitches that looked way more secure than they were. All this time the governor's eyelids were closed and he kept making clicking sounds with his teeth, like a movie cowboy signaling his horse.

A deeper wave of darkness set in, night catching up with the storm. Tommy shook the batteries out of the radio and inserted them into a flashlight, which he pinned under one arm. When I asked why he didn't just turn on the cabin light, Malley said they didn't want to drain the houseboat's battery, which was running low.

"T.C., you don't look so great," she said.

"What're you talkin' about?"

"I've got some aspirin in my bag. It works on a fever."

Once more I couldn't believe what she was saying. She should have been *cheering* for the fever.

"I'm good," he said sullenly.

"Are not. Let me feel your forehead." When she took a step toward him, he bellowed at her to stay back.

"I said I'm fine!"

"Fine! Be an ass."

"Don't mess with me!" Tommy said. Then he raised his arm and shot out one of the cabin windows.

Malley sat down sobbing. You could see the bullet hole in the flapping sheet, and hear the raindrops peppering the fabric. My ears rang, and I smelled the tang of gunpowder.

"Such drama," Skink said.

Tommy was completely frazzled. He was trying his hardest to scare a man who couldn't be scared.

"Know what? Maybe I should just kill you and Captain No-Beard. Dump you both overboard."

"Well, that would be labor-intensive," the governor responded, "not to mention messy. Your smarter option is to get a grip."

Tommy lurched close and placed the pistol to Skink's weed-capped head. "What'd you say, old man?"

"Don't!" Malley cried.

"See, she knows me. She knows what I can do," Tommy boasted, but he was trembling so much that the flashlight beam coming from his armpit jiggled all over the walls.

The revolver wasn't moving that much because Tommy was pressing it hard against Skink's temple.

One time I asked my father, who was super-laid-back, if he believed in evil. We'd been watching the TV news when an awful story came on about some guy who went to a crowded movie theater and started shooting everyone, people he'd never met before, even kids. The place looked like a war zone after he was done. The lawyer for the shooter said he had severe emotional problems (which was, like, no kidding), but in my mind that didn't account for how and why he devised a plan so awful and cold-blooded.

And I remember Dad mulling my question for a few moments before saying that true evil was rare, but, yes, it was real. He also said that it didn't occur in any other species besides humans, and I believe he was right. Violence and brutal domination exist in the animal world as a means for survival, not as sport or sick amusement.

Whatever personal issues Tommy Chalmers might have had during his life, it was a streak of pure evil that made him go after my cousin. I felt that way then, and I still do.

Poking Skink with the pistol barrel, Tommy said, "Well, old man? What do you think now?"

"I think you remind me of someone."

"Who's that?"

"The last fool who pointed a gun in my direction."

Tommy was on the verge of exploding.

My cousin said, "T.C., you're gonna ruin everything. Just chillax."

"What! Don't you hear how he's talkin' to me?"

"So what? He's nutty as a fruitcake."

"Ouch," said the governor.

Another crash of thunder rattled a wedge of glass from the shot-out windowpane. Malley used the distraction to scoot closer, and I felt her arm reaching behind me. At first I thought she was trying to loosen the knots, but actually she was placing an object in one of my hands.

It was the pocketknife from my backpack. She must have secretly removed it while retrieving the rope out of the hatch.

Tommy looked shakier by the minute. He backed away from Skink and braced himself against the frame of the doorway.

I said, "Just let us go, dude. Then you can get on with your cruise."

He shook his head, muttering, "Too late for that. No way. Too late." The flashlight flickered the way cheap ones do.

The governor turned slightly toward Malley. "How'd you two meet?"

Like we were all sitting in a booth at Applebee's, waiting for our salads.

"He found me in a chat room," my cousin said.

Tommy didn't care for the insinuation that he was some kind of stalker. He said, "Hey, babe, get it right. Who found who?"

"They're getting married in a couple days," I cut in. "Tommy's a poet. He wrote the wedding vows himself."

"Sweet," said Skink.

"He's looking for a word that rhymes with orange."

"Don't be a dorkface," Tommy snapped.

"He made it sound like we had a ton in common," Malley went on. "YOLO and so forth."

"YOLO?" said the governor.

"It stands for 'you only live once,'" I explained.

"Ah."

"My mom and dad were sending me off to boarding school," Malley said, "up in freaking New Hampshire. The more I thought about it, the more it sounded like a prison sentence. I don't do cold, okay? So then Tommy—he was calling himself 'Talbo' online—came up with this radical idea. He said hey, girl, why don't we just take off together, you and me. A trip to the middle of nowhere. And I said let's go for it."

This was the first time I'd heard my cousin tell the story, and it sounded about right.

"Well, you picked a fine river," Skink said. "There's a

special bird lives here that can't be found anywhere else in the country. Make that the entire planet."

Malley smiled. "You're talkin' about ivorybills. I saw one." She glanced at me. "It was *amazing*."

I assumed she said this because Tommy had overheard her talking about the woodpeckers when she'd called to give me a clue to her whereabouts—back when we both had working cell phones and laptops, when we were actually connected to the rest of civilization. It seemed like a long time ago.

"Young Thomas," said Skink, "what happened to your nose?"

"Some dirtbag sucker-punched me and I had to kick his butt. It's none a your flippin' business."

"You a North Florida boy? I am, too."

"Get me some water," Tommy said to Malley.

"She mentioned you called yourself 'Talbo' in the chit-chat room. That a family nickname?" The governor's tone was perfectly harmless.

"Talbo Chock. He was a friend of mine got killed in Iraq."

"Afghanistan," I said.

Skink nodded. "Always sad to hear that."

"He was in the Marines," added Tommy.

"You guys serve together?"

"Naw."

Malley poured water into Tommy's mouth, since he

couldn't hold the bottle with his catfish hand. If it was me, I might have grabbed for his gun, though I understood why she didn't. If she'd missed, he likely would have started shooting again.

In the meantime, I'd opened my knife, and I was making progress on the rope. Skink kept the conversation rolling. "Are your folks coming to the wedding?"

"What for? God, no," said Tommy.

"It's a big day, that's why. I've never been married myself."

"Who cares?"

"Never married?" Malley said. "Why not?"

The governor laughed and laughed. "There's a great song called 'Heart of Gold,' and that's what it would take to be married to me—someone with a heart of pure gold. Your parents know the words."

"I've heard it," I said.

"Me, too," said my cousin.

"Seriously? Shut up!" Tommy croaked. He was fighting tremors that made his shoulders pinch.

Skink asked Tommy how old he was and got no answer.

"He's twenty-four," Malley said.

"Old enough to know a blue heron isn't a game bird, right? Meaning it's against the law to kill one. A duck or a bobwhite quail—that's different. But there's no hunting season on herons."

The governor was hung up on the bird that Tommy almost shot. I sensed that he put Tommy in the same sleazy category as Dodge Olney, the turtle-egg poacher.

"Ever been to jail?" Skink inquired.

"Maybe I have," said Tommy, trying to sound proud of it.

"How about your father? Possibly there's a genetic explanation."

"My old man's a saint. Just ask him."

At this point I was sawing vigorously on the rope, hoping I didn't accidentally cut my wrists. I couldn't actually see what the knife was doing behind me.

My cousin brought up Tommy's supposed career as a big-time party DJ, which made no impression at all on Skink.

"The only DJs I ever heard were on the radio," he said.

"You mean, like, when, back in the Stone Age?" Tommy sniped.

The situation inside was heading downhill. Outside, the storm gave no signs of letting up. Skink began to croon the heart-of-gold song. He had an okay voice, but Tommy wasn't in the mood for a serenade.

Another powerful gust of wind came up the river swinging the bow hard, only this time the bow didn't swing back. The houseboat continued to spin.

"We just lost our anchor," Skink casually announced.

It was true. We were bobbing down the Choctawhatchee like a waterlogged cork. Tommy swore loudly. He ordered Malley to start the engine, and make it fast.

Just then the knots binding me went slack under a hard stroke of the blade. I kept my arms in the same position so Tommy wouldn't notice I was free. He was busy at the control console coaching my cousin, who pretended to be totally baffled by the ignition switch.

Slowly I slid the pocketknife behind Skink, and he palmed it. Time had run out for Malley's kidnapper.

Or so I thought.

SEVENTEEN

The engine wouldn't start.

Tommy Chalmers didn't know that the houseboat was equipped with a bilge pump that automatically switched on whenever water accumulated. The pump had been running nonstop during the heavy squall, draining so much juice from the boat's battery that there wasn't enough left to spark the big outboard.

"Unbelievable!" Tommy seethed. "You *got* to be kidding." For a moment I thought he might put a bullet in the ignition switch.

Malley sighed and stepped away from the controls. "Hey, I'm done. This is not my deal."

The governor said, "We're all part of something bigger now. Enjoy the drift."

At any moment I expected to see him shake off the rope and pounce on Tommy. I wondered if he would use my knife or only his bare hands. My cousin must have been anticipating a scuffle, too. She moved to a corner of the cabin, took off the bush hat and sat down on her travel bag.

"This is no good, Malley!" Tommy kicked the steering console. "Can you say total flippin' disaster?"

Skink waited until Tommy calmed down before asking why his right hand was wrapped in a bloody T-shirt. Tommy refused to answer, so Malley provided a brief account of the catfish episode.

"Been there," said Skink with a sympathetic wince.

Tommy grunted. "Who cares?"

"He won't let me put any medicine on it," Malley said.

"Why not?" the governor asked. "Tommy, are you a fan of pain?"

"No, he's just stubborn."

Tommy positioned the flashlight on the console with the feeble beam aimed at us. I peeked behind Skink and observed the knife blade going back and forth.

When he makes his big move, I thought, it'll be epic. Already I was imagining a triumphant phone call to my mother: *We got Malley back! She's okay!* I could picture Uncle Dan and Aunt Sandy rushing out of the house when we pulled up. They'd be crying and hugging my cousin so hard that her eyes would bulge. I could see myself down at the police station, telling Detective Trujillo how the rescue went down—he'd be totally blown away.

But back in real time, in the real world, Tommy Chalmers still held a loaded gun, and Skink still sat there wearing a crown of green waterweeds and a snail shell crammed into one eye socket. Lightning crackled around us as the houseboat spun in slow motion, pushed by the storm and pulled by the river's current.

And my cousin, for reasons known only to her, decided to stir things up even more. "T.C., there's something we should tell you."

"Who's we?" Tommy asked.

I had no idea what Malley was going to say. Looking back, I guess I shouldn't have been surprised. She wanted Tommy to know he'd been outwitted.

Matter-of-factly she announced, "Carson's real name is Richard. He's the cousin I told you about."

Tommy needed a few seconds to process the information.

"What the hell's he doing here?" he huffed.

"What do you think? He came to save me from you."

"Okay, that's bull. Nobody knew which way we went! I made sure a that."

"Well, he found us, didn't he?" Malley said. "See, some people really care, T.C. They don't just fake it. It's called a conscience."

Tommy blinked sweat beads off his eyelashes. "And some people don't slug their boyfriends in the nose."

"You're not my boyfriend. You were *never* my boyfriend."

"Ha! Yeah, right." He turned a bloodshot glare on me. "I never bought your stupid story. I knew you definitely didn't steal no yacht and run for Cuba. What about him, the old man?"

I said, "He's just a friend who offered to help."

"You lie. Look at him—he's a bum off the street!"

"Very classy, T.C.," said Malley. "Like you're one of the Kennedys. Or maybe you're a royal and you just forgot to tell me. Prince Thomas Chalmers of Kensington Palace, right?"

Now she was doing her British accent, but with a nasty edge.

Skink said, "I take no offense at the man's remarks. Often I'm misjudged due to my appearance."

I thought: *Enough talking already*. He had finished cutting himself free. I could see the rope in pieces behind him, the pocketknife twirling in his fingers.

"He looks like some hobo got run over by a train!" Tommy chortled.

"Actually, it was a truck," I said.

"Partially run over," Skink added for clarification, "although I make no excuses."

My cousin reminded Tommy that he looked awfully sketchy himself. "You're one to talk, with your fat nose and club hand!"

It was like pouring gasoline on a fire, but that's how Malley's anger was coming out, as sarcastic digs.

"Don't listen to him—he's just jealous," Malley said to the governor. "You've got epic teeth. Do you whiten?"

"Pardon?"

"Crest strips, right?"

"I floss like a fiend," Skink replied with a straight face, "sometimes using barbed wire."

"Okay, that's it. Let's move on," I said.

What I wanted was the night to be over. Even wracked with fever, Tommy was able to comprehend that he couldn't allow me and Skink to leave. You can't just tie up a couple of strangers, wave a gun in their faces and then say never mind, see ya later. They're going to call the cops as soon as they can.

We were eyewitnesses to a crime, Skink and I, which meant Tommy either had to keep us as prisoners or kill us.

"How'd you find out where we were?" he asked. "Did she tell you?"

"No, I traced your cell phone signal. There's an app called triangulated telemetry."

Which sounded totally legit, even though I'd just made it up. Tommy seemed semi-persuaded until Malley butted in again.

"He's full of crap, T.C. I told him where we were," she said. "We had a code on the phone. Isn't that right, Richard?"

I stared at her wordlessly. What I wanted to say was: *Are you out of your mind? You want to get us all shot?*

"Would a real 'girlfriend' pull that sorta thing, T.C.?" my cousin went on. "Rat you out? No way! Because I wasn't *ever* your girlfriend, so quit saying I was. 'Triangulated telemetry,' are you freakin' serious?"

In a husky voice Tommy said: "What kinda code?"

Skink stood up, grumbling, "You youngsters are giving me a migraine." He continued to keep his hands behind him. Tommy, who didn't notice the rope fragments on the floor, ordered him to sit back down.

"Relax, son. What have you got to fear from a broken old street bum like me?" The governor was so tall that he had to stoop slightly inside the houseboat. "Just stretchin' my legs," he said.

"Sit your ass down. Final warning." Tommy aimed the pistol at Skink's heart, and for a sick man his arm seemed very steady. Frighteningly steady.

Malley was biting her lower lip. "Don't make things worse, T.C."

He gave a hollow laugh. "Worse than this? Not possible, babe."

That's when I stood up, too—not a hero move, I promise. When the governor lunged for Tommy (which I hoped would happen any second), my intention was to grab my cousin and get both of us out of there.

Skink said, "Thomas, let's review why your integrity is being questioned."

"Let's not," he snapped.

"You took advantage of this young lady's situation, her problems at home, by luring her into accompanying you on this trip. To make a personal connection you hid behind a false name, the identity of a young Marine who died in combat—a hoax on your part that personally I find unforgivable."

"Say one more word, old man, you're dead. Talbo Chock was my best friend ever!"

"Then tell me the name of the cemetery where he's buried. Surely you attended the funeral."

"I don't remember. It was Our Lady of the Blessed something."

"Wrong."

Tommy was busted and he knew it. He shivered wretchedly but he didn't lower the pistol.

"I'm not a deeply religious person," Skink continued, "but stealing a preacher's car is a slime-dog move, even by the gutter standards of today's common criminal. I presume this houseboat was obtained the same way—by theft rather than an honest purchase."

"It's a loaner," Tommy said dully.

"No, he stole it," Malley interjected, "in the middle of the night. After he sunk the car, we hitched a ride to some marina and jumped the fence."

Skink brought his freed hands out from behind his back. No pocketknife.

You're kidding me, I thought.

"Son," he said to Tommy, "you've chosen the proverbial dead-end highway. Anyone who takes pot shots at a lovely wading bird is a hopeless defective, in my view, an evolutionary mistake. There's a natural order to what happens to you next, an inevitable conclusion to all this low villainy."

It was quite a performance. Dodge Olney probably

heard the same sort of lecture before he wound up in the ambulance.

Tommy wore a crooked, clueless grin. "Oh yeah? Well, here's *my* conclusion. I'm gonna kill all three of you and dump your dead bodies in the river."

"No, you are NOT!" Malley was beet-faced, shaking a fist. "You've done enough, T.C. Too much!"

Skink parted the sheet and used a frayed edge to wipe a circle in the condensation on the windshield. Peering downstream he said, "By the way, Thomas, there *is* a word that rhymes with orange. 'Sporange.' S-p-o-r-a-n-ge. The definition can be found in the unabridged Oxford dictionary. I'd say go look it up, except you won't have the opportunity."

Tommy cocked the pistol's hammer maybe two seconds before the houseboat struck the half-submerged tree stump that Skink must have spotted ahead of us when he looked through the window. The boat shuddered, swayed—then the gun went off. Blue light flashed from the muzzle, and the bang was deafening.

The governor didn't go down. He was on top of Tommy in an instant, yelling for me and Malley to get off the bleeping boat. I dragged her breathless and squirming through the cabin door. Outside in a stinging rain I pulled her close and told her everything was all right. She was shuddering, weeping into the front of my shirt. I'd never seen her that way before, and I won't lie. It shook me up.

Skink appeared, hauling Tommy by the hair and backlit

by the strobing flashlight, which was rolling around the floor of the cabin. Once again the old man had been lucky, the bullet barely grazing an ear lobe. He hurled something overboard, and from the heavy splash I knew it was the gun.

"Okay, let's go! Let's go!" I screamed.

"With no further delay," he said in that canyon-deep rumble, and with a gentle sweep of an arm he launched me and my cousin over the side, into the muddy roiling Choctawhatchee.

Malley and I are both good swimmers, but swimming for fun is way different than swimming for your life. We got to shore, but you wouldn't call it graceful. Like two weary frogs we shimmied up the slick bank and hugged the trunk of a cypress, flinching at every thunderclap.

I turned my head so I could see the houseboat. It was drifting away at a peculiar tilt, pulling the canoe like a sleek dog on a leash. A familiar wide-shouldered silhouette remained visible on the aft deck. He'd been watching to make sure Malley and I had made it. I called out his name, but of course he wasn't coming.

A fork of lightning split the clouds, a phenomenal silver-yellow pulse that froze Skink in place like the flash from an old-time camera. One arm was raised skyward, the hand open in a farewell wave. At the end of his other arm hung the thrashing, raging form of Tommy Chalmers.

The governor's smile seemed to cast its own light.

That insane movie-star smile.

I swear I could still see it after the sky went black.

EIGHTEEN

During the storm I fell fast asleep. Incredible but true.

Scared stiff, plastered to a tree, soaked to the bone, thunder booming, Malley huddled at my side. . . .

Not only did I sleep, I had a dream, which I blame on watching too much TV with my stepfather. A Bigfoot was chasing me through the parking lot of an Applebee's. It wasn't your standard Bigfoot, all hairy and ape-like. This one was scaly and pink and stunk like a garfish, though it was wearing a really sweet pair of Oakley shades. Trent would have been blown away. The Bigfoot didn't look like Tommy Chalmers, but instead it was a dead ringer for Mrs. Curbside, my seventh-grade Language Arts teacher. FYI, in real life Mrs. Curbside weighs maybe a hundred pounds.

The dream Bigfoot didn't ever catch me, but I felt worn out when I woke up. There was rapid tapping, like a drum roll, on the tree trunk. I could feel the vibration in my fingertips. Malley was sitting on the bank trying to dry her sneakers. Her soaked hoodie lay in a heap beside her.

She said, "See? I really saw one."

"Saw what?"

"Shh. Don't spook him."

I followed her gaze up the branches to where a tall red-crested woodpecker was drilling holes in the bark. It was a cloudless morning, so the bird's dark feathers stood out vividly against the pale sky.

"Mal, that's not an ivorybill," I whispered.

"Is too!"

"There's no white down its back. And check out the beak," I said. "It's too dark and pointy. That's a male pileated."

"You're wrong, Richard."

The woodpecker quit drumming and cocked its head to scope us out. I wished it had been an ivorybill, but it wasn't.

"Still very cool," I said to my cousin.

She snorted. "You think you know everything."

The bird gave several high-pitched squawks and took off. I sat down beside Malley and removed my own wet sneakers. Above us the tree limbs looked stark except for wispy flags of Spanish moss that reminded me of the governor's beard. In front of us the Choctawhatchee rolled high and fast, creamy with mud. Overnight it had carried the damaged houseboat downstream, and possibly engulfed it.

"Decision time, Richard. Do we stay here or make a run for it?"

There was a third option, too, but I said, "Let's wait here for some fishermen to come along. Somebody'll have a phone we can use."

"But what about your one-eyed, leech-slurping friend?"

"I know." Skink wouldn't want us to go searching for him, though Malley and I were both thinking about it.

"There's a reason he shoved us off the boat," I said.

"Something really bad could happen to him. Tommy's totally whacked."

"Tommy's in over his head."

I told her some of what I knew about Skink, starting with Vietnam. How later he was elected governor, got depressed, freaked out and disappeared. How he lives off eating roadkill. How he lost his left eye to thugs. I mentioned there were crazy rumors on the Internet, but nobody could prove a thing. I told her about him fighting the turtle-egg robber on the beach, about the gray getaway car that mysteriously had been left in town for him. How it was his idea to come save her from T.C. How his foot got run over when was he saving the baby skunk.

I ended with a description of the canoe being pulled away by a gigantic alligator, Skink plunging in after it.

My cousin said, "God, but he's so *old*. He's, like, older than Grandpa Ed, and Grandpa Ed couldn't wrestle a gecko."

"The governor's a serious freak of nature."

"You think he's gonna hurt Tommy?"

"That'll depend on Tommy's attitude."

"I hope he does," she said. "Hurt him. Does that sound terrible? I don't care."

"Did Tommy hurt *you*?"

The sun was sneaking over the treetops, warming our

arms and legs. Malley was braiding her hair into two long strands, scowling at the black dye job.

"He kissed me a couple times," she said, "which I told him to knock off. When he didn't, I slugged him in the nose. You should've seen the mess, like a rotten tomato exploded on his face. After that was when he brought out the handcuffs."

"What else?" I asked.

"Online he came across so different, so . . . normal. And not mean at all. He emailed me this one poem—'a daughter of the gods, divinely tall, and most divinely fair.' Said he wrote it late one night just for me, and like an airhead I'm all, 'Oh, Talbo, that's so sweet!'

"Then he picks me up at the airport in Orlando, and after a day or two he isn't sounding so much like a great poet. So I Google a few lines of his masterpiece and guess what? He stole it from Alfred Lord Tennyson, or Lord Alfred Tennyson, whatever. Some English writer who died like a hundred years ago. I called Tommy out on it, and that's when he smashed my laptop. I was so pissed."

"When did you find out he wasn't Talbo Chock?"

My cousin smiled ruefully. "I busted him on that deal right away. Lots of people use weird screen names, so it didn't seem like a biggie. But, seriously, I had no idea the real Talbo was a soldier, swear to God. Turns out there's lots of stuff about T.C. I didn't know."

"Like the poet was driving a stolen car?"

"Yeah. I figured that out when he decided to sink it."

"What else happened? What else did he do?" I asked.

"I'm fine. Stop worrying, you sound like Dad."

"Let me see your wrists."

"He always made the handcuffs too tight. He said he bought 'em at a gun show."

Behind Malley was a stand of wild azaleas, the leaves yellow and pale orange. It was a peaceful burst of color.

"Know what I feel really bad about?" she said. "The beer and gas we brought back in the canoe—Tommy swiped all that from a house trailer on a lot about a mile down the river. The ice cubes, too. I said why don't we leave these people some money, and he just laughed."

"I still feel bad about Saint Augustine. Same thing."

"Richard, that was so *not* the same thing. You were just freaked about losing your dad. I mean, dude, you don't even like to skateboard."

"Stealing is stealing."

She said, "Hey, I'm really sorry I ever brought it up. I'd never, *ever* in a jillion years tell your mother, okay? But I had to say whatever so you wouldn't rat me out, even though you did anyway, until I was far away. The scene at home, I don't know, I was just ultra-stressed and I had to shake free. You understand? Talbo—I mean Tommy—he was my ticket out. Big mistake, no doubt. *Major* mistake. But, God, Mom was on my case all the time and Dad's always takin' her side—no way am I going to school at the Twirp Academy! Sorry, sports fans. A New Hampshire winter is *not* on this girl's wish list."

Another blue heron glided low across the Choctaw-hatchee trailing its stick-thin legs the way they do. I knew it wasn't the same one Tommy Chalmers had fired at. That poor critter was probably halfway to Mexico, and still flying.

Malley went on: "He told me he understood everything I was going through. He said we'd just be good friends and not to worry—if I changed my mind about running away, he'd turn the car around and drive me straight home. That's what he promised, word for word. I was so beyond stupid to believe him."

"That's what liars are pro at, making people believe them."

"I know, right? Tommy had the nice-guy act totally down."

"Still, not a genius move on your part," I said, "taking off with a stranger you met in a chat room."

"I really thought I could handle him, but what a psycho. That whole wedding-on-the-beach thing? Perv World."

The river life was waking up. We saw a fat sturgeon jump, about as graceful as a flying log. Ospreys were on patrol calling to each other. Our gaze turned downriver, and so did our thoughts.

"That old man gets hurt or killed, it's all on me," Malley said. "If he ends up dead, I'll hate myself forever."

"Don't worry. He threw the pistol overboard."

She looked downcast. "Tommy's got another one."

"Don't tell me that."

"He stashed it somewhere on the boat. He didn't want

me to see where, 'cause he said I'd 'cap' him if I got the chance, but no way. Guns scare the pee out of me, Richard. Speaking of which, I can't believe you jumped T.C. after he shot at that bird! You went all Vin Diesel on him!"

"Another opposite-of-genius move," I said.

It was bad news that Tommy Chalmers had stashed a second gun aboard. I told myself everything would work out all right—Tommy was weakened and woozy from the catfish infection. He probably wouldn't even remember where he hid the pistol on the houseboat.

Was the houseboat even still afloat? If so, probably not for long.

Skink would know when it was time to abandon ship. Would he take Tommy with him? I could totally picture the governor coming out of the river alone, the kidnapper's body being found days later in the sunken wreck.

Or never seen again.

From what Skink had told me about his life, I knew he was capable of such things. I also suspected that he wasn't one to exaggerate.

Malley was growing restless on the riverbank. "How will we get somebody to stop and pick us up?"

"Uh, we yell 'Help'?"

"Not funny, Richard."

"I'm serious. That's what marooned people do."

She made a snarky face. "So not cool."

This was my cousin in full-on diva mode—too vain to call for help. Unbelievable.

"Then yell 'Asparagus!' if you want," I said. "I'm yelling 'Help!'"

As it turned out, we didn't get a chance to yell anything. Two hours passed without a single boat appearing on the Choctawhatchee. The fishermen were staying home because the river was too churned from the storm. So far I hadn't seen one osprey make a dive, which meant that even full-time fishing birds couldn't find any fish. Only the occasional leaping sturgeon broke the surface.

I told Malley we'd better get moving.

"Which way?"

"Back toward the highway bridge where Skink parked. We'll walk close to the shoreline in case a boat comes by."

"Richard, you do see it's a total swamp, right? Thanks to that insane rain."

"It was swampy *before* the rain," I said.

"Yeah, what if I want to go the other way?"

"Be my guest. Maybe you'll find a paved bike path with water fountains."

"Sometimes you're such an ass," said Malley.

"Hurry, put on your shoes."

She went ahead of me, taking long, show-offy strides. We definitely weren't in ninja mode—more like two buffaloes splashing through a rice paddy. Not that we were trying to sneak up on anything, just the opposite. We *wanted* to be heard and seen, preferably by a friendly human who could lead us to safety.

The hiking would have gone easier if we'd had higher,

drier ground, but the deep woods that lay ahead of us were low-lying and boggy. The sticky air buzzed with gnats, mosquitoes and small biting flies. I couldn't find any wax myrtle leaves to crush and wipe on our skin.

Hooked to her iPod earbuds, Malley could go forever. Without her music she quickly got bored and cranky. After a while I ignored the complaining, though I was tempted to say: *Would you rather be back on the boat with your maniac kidnapper?*

As thirsty as we were, neither of us would drink the murky river water. The last thing we needed on our trek was an attack of jungle diarrhea. We grew tired in the heat, and our pace slowed down. Rest breaks became more frequent. We got good at slapping insects off of each other without leaving a mark.

The sun was almost dead high, so cool patches of shade got harder to find. In the brutal humidity my cousin and I were panting like old hound dogs.

"How long till we get there?" she asked.

"I don't know. A while longer."

"This sucks, Richard."

The next time we stopped it was pretty much the same conversation. The time after that, Malley got superexcited and said she heard an ambulance siren, which meant we must be nearing the highway. While I wanted that to be true, I couldn't hear anything except the rattle of cicadas in the bushes. She got mad at me, of course, and declared that we should immediately turn due west because that's where the sound of the ambulance had come from. I said no.

"Who made you the navigator?" she huffed.

"I'm older."

"By only nine stupid days!"

"Come on, Mal, it's a joke. Let's keep walking."

My cousin isn't a patient person, but extreme patience is what the situation called for. It's not as if we were lost. The Road 20 bridge wasn't going anywhere, and we didn't need a GPS to find it. All we had to do was follow the shoreline of the Choctawhatchee upstream. I didn't want to be too harsh with Malley, after all she'd been through, but there was no way I'd let her take charge of our escape.

The last time we stopped to rest, I was the one who heard a noise.

"Somebody's following us."

"Okay, you're finally losing it, Richard."

"Please shut up and listen."

"It's probably a deer. They're thick around here."

"Not a deer," I said. "A deer would be running the other way."

Something definitely was approaching us from behind, moving with zero stealth through the tangled cover and rain puddles. My first emotion was relief, because I thought it had to be the governor—the houseboat had sunk and he'd made it to shore and was trying to find us.

"Hey, Skink!" I shouted. "This way!"

Nobody shouted back.

"It's Richard! We're over here!"

Still no voice answered from the woods. Malley and I stood up.

"Now I hear him," she whispered.

The splash of footfalls, the snapping of twigs and a muffled snort, like a man trying to swallow a laugh.

I thought of Tommy Chalmers and my stomach pitched. What if he'd gotten hold of the second gun and shot Skink? What if he alone made it off the sinking boat, and now he was stalking me and my cousin?

She looked at me anxiously. "Well?"

"I say let's wait and see."

"I say let's run."

There was no time to continue the discussion because our stalker had materialized like a glistening ghost at the edge of the clearing. He was hunched forward, slobbering and gape-jawed, his black eyes narrowed in fury.

"This is *not* happening," Malley said in a cracked voice.

"Don't panic," I told her, which was idiotic. Panic was the only logical reaction.

"Richard?"

"Yeah?"

"Can I run now?"

"Yes, run."

And I was right behind her.

NINETEEN

One man was to blame for our present dilemma, and it wasn't Tommy Chalmers.

It was Hernando de Soto, the Spanish explorer. He is most famous for discovering the Mississippi River, but he did something else on his historic expedition that caused Malley and me to be running for our lives nearly five centuries later, along the banks of a different river.

On May 25, 1539, de Soto's flotilla sailed into Tampa Bay and pitched camp. The conquistador and his soldiers had crossed the sea carrying weapons, ammo, supplies and, for food, thirteen pigs. These were the very first pigs ever to set foot (hoof, actually) on the North American continent, and from the beginning the sturdy oinkers made it clear that they didn't miss Europe one bit.

If de Soto had brought cows or even goats to the New World, my cousin and I wouldn't have been in such deep trouble. Goats and cows are grazing animals, content to hang out in a pasture and mind their own business. Not pigs. Pigs require supervision, because they're so curious and crafty, adaptable to almost every type of habitat. They totally loved Florida, and since happy grownup pigs produce lots of baby pigs, de Soto's pack multiplied faster than he and his men could barbecue.

For three years the Spanish forces tramped through the southeastern wilderness terrorizing, torturing and enslaving the native Indians. This was standard operating procedure back in those days, though it doesn't make de Soto any less of a cruel thug. Who knows how much more misery he would have inflicted on the locals if he hadn't caught a fever and croaked. It happened soon after he reached the Mississippi, by which time his imported pig herd had grown to seven hundred slobbering mouths.

Flash forward to the twenty-first century and a sprawling country that's been settled from coast to coast—a country that craves a fat, juicy pork chop. Pigs are a huge business in America, raised and slaughtered by the millions. Over the decades, however, many have escaped from farm pens and scuttled into the woods, where they've become as wild as bobcats or coyotes—only bigger, and way more destructive.

I researched all this myself later, though not for a new science project. I was simply curious to know all about the badass creature that nearly killed me.

These so-called feral pigs now roam forty-five states and they party hard, destroying valuable crops and wetlands with their sloppy rooting. Some places have officially declared war on free-roaming swine and offer cash bounties to hunters. So far, the swine are winning.

The boar chasing Malley and me must've weighed at least two hundred pounds, and that's no lie. His long black nose was bristly, and his nappy thick fur was the color of a rusted junkyard heap. He owned two sets of filthy yellowed tusks, the bottom pair being longer and more curved. My goal was to avoid finding out how sharp they were.

Malley was way ahead, weaving through trees, hurtling the scrub, bounding over puddles. It was ridiculous, she was so much faster than me. Every few strides she'd glance back to see if I was catching up, and I'd yell at her to keep running. "Don't slow down! Go! Go!"

The wild pig huffed like a locomotive at my heels. His shoulders were low to the ground, and he kept slashing his tusks in an upward motion that would have sliced the tendons in my legs, had I faltered. Only later did I learn that a boar that size can reach a speed of thirty miles an hour, much fleeter than any human, which explained why he seemed to be moving at such an easy trot.

Optimistically I surmised that he wasn't interested in eating me for breakfast (pigs will eat *anything*), but rather that he only wished to drive us out of his territory. Malley and I would have happily departed with no further encouragement, yet the beast continued his cold-eyed pursuit. If it had been a movie, Nickel the gar man would have stepped out of the bushes and plugged the pig with his .22. Then he would have grinned at me and said, "See, boy? Dint I warn you 'bout them things?"

But that wasn't going to happen. There was no sign

of Nickel and now, ahead of me, no sign of my track-star cousin. She'd left me in the dust (well, the muck), which is what I'd urged her to do. No sense in both of us getting mauled.

My lungs burned, my knees throbbed and I was painfully aware I'd never outrun the mad boar, undoubtedly a great-great-great-great-great-great-great-great-great-great-great-grandson of a seafaring de Soto piglet.

I decided to climb a tree. No big deal, right?

Wrong. Not all trees are designed for rapid climbing, and the good ones are scarce when you absolutely, positively need to reach a safe altitude. Try scaling an ancient bald cypress when the trunk is slick from a rainstorm or the nearest boughs are too high to offer a step. It's a sure way to end up flat on your back, staring up a hairy pair of cavernous pig nostrils.

So onward I ran until spying a young maple that forked conveniently at a height of maybe five feet. I scaled straight up the bark, wedged a foot into that snug cleft and slapped both hands around a sturdy branch. With a tired grunt I pulled myself into the tree's leafy embrace and there I balanced, huffing to catch my breath. Below, the wild boar swiped his tusks back and forth across the trunk, sharpening their edges with each long scrape.

Hang in there, I told myself. *He'll get bored soon and go away.*

Then the demon pig did the one thing I didn't expect. He lay down panting and closed his eyes.

"You're kidding," I said out loud.

My mood was not good. I was desperately thirsty, sore, itchy, exhausted, worried about Malley being alone in the forest. . . .

And now the swine was taking a nap under my maple tree.

I said, "No. Way."

The critter began to snore, his upper lip flapping slightly. He reminded me of Trent dozing on the sofa in front of our TV.

I considered jumping down from the tree, but I feared the sound of my landing would rouse the boar and spark another chase. A second choice was to stay patient and pray that the smelly porker would wake up and wander away, having forgotten what had led him to that spot. Unfortunately, a pig that size could sleep all day, and I didn't have the whole day to waste. I didn't even have an hour.

My cousin wasn't blessed with a flawless sense of direction, and all the foot-speed in the world wouldn't help if she made a wrong turn. She had no water or food, and the midday heat was hellish. Another unpleasant issue was snakes. Malley was accustomed to running safe ovals on our school's bright, smooth, reptile-free track. But the Choctawhatchee River basin was basically snake heaven, and it would be easy to accidentally step on a murky-colored water moccasin.

I didn't want to think about Malley getting snakebit all by herself, lost and miles from a hospital. Instead I focused on my problem porker, who was drifting deep into piggy dreamland. The new plan was to startle him so badly that he'd jump up and gallop off, freeing me to go find Malley. Working in my favor (or so I thought) was the element of surprise.

My family used to have a beagle-setter mix named Slater who would freak out if anyone tried to pet him while he was asleep. I mean, this dog would whip around and snap like crazy. Yet when he was awake, he was the chillest, friendliest little dude you ever met. Dad said he had a college roommate who was the same way, a total bundle of nerves once his head hit the pillow. You couldn't make a sound in the dorm room because you didn't know how he might react. One night, as a joke, my father and another student put a live gerbil on the sleeping kid's bed, and he leaped naked and yowling out the window. Luckily, the room was on the first floor.

I was hoping for a similar reaction from the dozing boar. Reaching down, I gingerly tugged the soggy sneaker from my right foot. Then I took aim.

In Little League I played shortstop, a position that requires a strong, accurate arm. Although I wasn't much of a hitter, I could definitely throw some heat. The sneaker struck the pig with a wet smack flush on the tip of his quivering, disgustingly runny nose.

Sadly for me, the brute didn't bolt wide awake and race off in a panic.

Instead he groggily rose, grunted twice, clacked his

tusks and hunched closer to examine the odd object that had bounced off of his face. It was a size-8 Nike cross-trainer with neon-lime soles and a silver swoosh on the sides, not that the pig cared about style.

To him my shoe was nothing but a snack, which he chewed up and swallowed with a rude gurgle.

"Perfect!" I yelled down from the branches. "Just perfect!"

The boar raised his anvil-sized noggin to peer at me.

"Get outta here! Go away!"

He didn't run. He didn't walk. He just yawned, unfurling his long pink slug of a tongue.

I hollered some more and shook the branches, Bigfoot-style. You've probably never seen a pig shrug, but they do. Trust me. I got so mad that I threw my other Nike, which he actually caught with his yellowed chompers. The sneaker was gone in two seconds, and the foul critter's tufted tail began to wag.

He thought it was a game!

"We're done here," I snapped, in sour defeat.

Cheerfully the boar circled the base of the maple tree waiting for another tasty shoe to hit him. There was no doubt in my mind that he could do that for hours.

"I AM SUCH AN IDIOT!" I shouted into the woods.

And, to my shock, the woods shouted back: "I've been tellin' you that since pre-K!"

My cousin, of course. She'd come back to get me. I spotted her crouching behind a spruce pine.

"Mal, don't do anything stupid!"

"You mean like feed my sneakers to a pig?"

"Stay back or he'll rip you to shreds."

Slowly she emerged from behind the tree. The boar stopped circling below me and squinted intently in her direction.

"Hey there, Mister Pig," said Malley.

The animal lifted his twitchy snout in the air. Pigs possess average eyesight but an amazing sense of smell.

"Oh great. It's your shoes," I said.

"Mine are Reeboks, not Nikes."

"He doesn't care."

"This is all your fault, Richard."

"Honestly? He'd eat a truck tire if you rolled it to him."

Malley took a dainty step forward and said, "You're such a nice piggy."

"He's *not* a nice piggy."

"Shut up, Richard."

"And he's faster than you think."

"Good mister pig," she said softly.

"You're wasting your breath."

The boar snorted and pawed at the dirt.

"Do you have a plan?" I asked my cousin.

"Just wait."

"You're only pissing him off."

"I so *do* have a plan," said Malley.

Then she began to dance, which was spectacularly weird because my cousin doesn't dance. Not with her girlfriends. Not with boys. Not even in the privacy of her own room—or so she says. At parties she refuses to grind, freak or twerk. The only rhythmic motion I've ever seen from her is her chin bobbing in time to music.

Which, at least then there was music. The woods of the Choctawhatchee were as silent as a graveyard, except for the heavy panting of the wild boar. From my tree perch I couldn't tell whether the animal was enraged or just confused.

It's almost impossible to describe the wild jerky moves that Malley was making, her black braids twirling like helicopter rotors, her pale eyes rolled back in the sockets. At first I thought she was having some sort of convulsion, then she started to sing.

If you could call it singing . . .

Yo, hog!
Go, hog!
You hip,
You hop.
I makin'
Some bacon.
So, yo, pig!
Slow pig!
Be gone,
Be quick,
Or you am,
Big ham!

It wasn't the words to Malley's song that frightened the wild boar. It was her crazed flailing and annoying off-key voice. In a lifetime of roaming the wilderness, that poor pig had probably never encountered anything so disturbing. I actually wasn't surprised to see him wheel around and sprint away. If Malley wasn't my cousin, I would have run, too.

"You can stop now!" I shouted.

"You're welcome," said Malley.

Shoeless, I climbed down from the maple and once more we set off for the bridge.

TWENTY

"Get in," I said.

"What do you think you're doing?"

"Just get in."

The plain gray Malibu was in the same place, at the east end of the bridge, where Skink and I had left it. I lifted the floor mat on the driver's side and grabbed the keys.

"Don't even," said Malley.

"Hey, I can drive now."

I popped the trunk and placed the shoe box inside. I'd been happily surprised to find it buried in the same hole beneath the tupelo tree, and even more surprised to feel the weight of the cash bundles. If Nickel the gar man had dug up the box, he must not have taken much of the money for his water-taxi fee.

"Richard, you so *don't* know how to drive."

"Oh yes, I do." I showed her the license that Mr. Tile had given me.

She snickered. "Who'd you have to bribe to get this?"

"It's legit, Mal."

"Liar. You're not old enough."

"You want to hitchhike? Me, neither." I positioned myself behind the steering wheel, centering my butt on the thick John Steinbeck novel.

"Well, you look like a total dork," my cousin remarked, but she still got in the car.

I turned the key in the ignition, and the Malibu rumbled to life. Malley shot me a tight sidewise look as she hastily buckled her seat belt.

"We need a phone," I said. Mine was in my backpack on the houseboat. Hers was in the river, where Tommy Chalmers had tossed it.

Hanging uselessly from a socket in the console of the Malibu was my battery charger.

Malley said, "Okay, Dale Jr., let's see what you got."

I slipped the transmission into Drive and took my right foot off the brake. We started to roll.

"Gee, I'm so impressed," said Malley.

"Would you shut up?" I was nervous enough without her sarcastic commentary.

Traffic on Road 20 was light, thank goodness. I waited until no vehicles were coming either way before I made a very careful, very slow U-turn. As soon as the car was lined up on the straightaway, I pushed down on the accelerator the way Skink had showed me, like stepping on an egg and trying not to break it.

"So, who taught you how?" Malley asked.

"The governor. After his foot got smashed."

"What's it like?"

"Fun," I said. "Scary at first."

She was watching me closely. I sensed she was a little envious. "You're doin' pretty good," she admitted.

"We'll see."

"I'm tall enough I wouldn't need to sit on a book."

"You're only two inches taller than me."

"Two and a half. Is it legal for you to drive barefoot?"

"We're in Walton County, Florida. I'm guessing the dress code's pretty chill."

"But what if—"

"What if you stop asking questions and start looking for a pay phone?" I said.

"A what?"

She spotted one outside a Tom Thumb store. A logging truck stacked with cut pines took up the entire parking lot, and I nearly had a heart attack trying to squeeze past it in the Malibu. For once Malley stayed quiet.

Neither of us had ever used a public telephone. It looked like something from a museum. I lifted the receiver, which reeked of cigarette smoke, and punched my mom's number into the gummy keypad. An operator came on the line asking how I wanted to pay for the call. Malley and I didn't have any coins, not one.

"My mother'll pay for it," I told the operator.

"So you'd like to reverse the charges?"

"Is that the same as calling collect?"

"Please hold on," she said.

After two rings I put the receiver back on the hook.

Malley gave me a quizzical look.

"What if we stayed one more day?" I asked.

"For what? Oh."

"He came back for you and me. We should go back for him."

"Once we tell the police about the houseboat, they'll get right on it," Malley said.

"You don't understand. Everyone thinks he's dead, and that's how he likes it. Certain things he's been involved with over the years—I mean, things they *think* he's been involved with—the cops'll have a ton of questions. Once they check his fingerprints and find out who he is . . ."

"It's that bad?"

"It's just messy," I said.

Skink wouldn't have approved the mission. He would've said my job was to get my cousin home as fast as possible. Yet what if he needed help down the river? What if he'd been hurt so badly that he couldn't get himself to a hospital?

I owed the man. He'd risked everything for Malley and me.

"If you're not up for it," I told her, "I totally understand. I can drop you at the police station."

"You try that and I'll kick your ass, Richard Sloan. This T.C. disaster is totally my fault." Malley reached for the telephone and slapped it in my hand. "So come up with a story that'll buy us some time to find your weird old senator."

"Governor."

"Whatever. Use your famous imagination."

But my imagination stalled. The best excuse I could think of was car trouble, which Malley said was incredibly weak. When the operator placed the call to my house, I lucked out and got the answering machine.

"Hey, Mom, it's me! We found Malley and she's okay and we're coming home. It's a long story, I can't wait to tell you what happened, but I lost my phone and now the car's overheating. Don't worry, though. Skink says he'll have us home tomorrow night. And please don't—"

"Sir? Excuse me, sir?" It was the operator.

"Yes?"

"You'll have to try again later. Nobody was there to accept the charges."

"But what about my message—"

"I had to disconnect as soon as the recording came on. There has to be a person on the other end to take the call."

"Hang on," I said, and handed the phone to my cousin. She gave the operator her home phone number.

Uncle Dan picked up on the first ring and practically shouted, "My God, of course we'll accept the charges!" Even standing several feet away I could hear the sobs on the other end, he was so excited to hear his daughter's voice. Aunt Sandy picked up on another line, and it was more of the same.

And Malley—cynical, selfish, tough-as-nails Malley— began crying, too.

I ducked around the corner to give her some privacy. She found me sitting on a curb near the Dumpster.

"We're good to go," she announced with a leftover sniffle.

"What story did you go with?"

"Never mind, Richard."

"Car trouble, I bet."

"Yeah, so what?"

"Ha!"

"Who did you tell them was driving us?"

"I said we found a cab driver in Panama City who'd do the trip for five hundred bucks plus gas. I said they can write him a check when we get home."

"Not bad," I admitted.

"I said the radiator in his taxi blew up, but it'll be fixed by tomorrow. They still have radiators, right?"

"Absolutely."

"Excellent," said Malley. "My mom's calling your mom right now."

"But no police yet, right?"

"Definitely. I told her all I want to do is come home and go to sleep in my own bed."

"Which happens to be true, right? You can say it, Mal."

"Give me some money."

At the Tom Thumb we bought a road map, a Styrofoam picnic cooler, five pounds of ice, twelve bottles of water, a six-pack of Coke, chocolate-chip cookies, a bag of Doritos, two prepackaged subs layered with anonymous gray meat, a box of granola bars and four random candy bars (excluding Butterfingers, because that's what my father was eating when he had his stupid accident).

I handed the tattooed store clerk a couple of damp fifty-dollar bills that I'd gotten from the shoe box. If he was suspicious, it didn't show. He gave me back twenty-two dollars and change, and said there was a restroom in the back, if we wanted to clean up.

Hint, hint.

Malley and I packed the cooler to the brim, hoisted it into the backseat of the Malibu and took off. I know you're supposed to drive with both hands, but I kept one off the wheel so I could stuff my face with snacks and guzzle a cold bottle of water. It was either that or pass out from hunger.

The map was spread open on Malley's lap, sprinkled with granola crumbs from the bar she was gnawing like a starved chipmunk.

"Go straight," she advised.

"Straight is good."

"Till you get to a place called Freeport, then hang a left. From there it's like four miles to the bay."

Choctawhatchee Bay, where the river empties.

I glanced at the speedometer and nearly choked. Sixty-six miles an hour! That's what happens when you're in a super hurry—your foot gets heavy on the pedal and you don't even realize it. I tapped the brake until the needle dropped to fifty, which Skink had told me was the ideal pace for blending with traffic. Driving too slowly, he'd said, attracts just as much attention as driving too fast.

"Beth really likes you," my cousin said, out of nowhere. That's how I knew she was anxious with me behind the wheel—she was trying to make small talk, act casual.

"No way," I said. "Beth's going with Taylor."

"He's a loser. You should call her. She's hot, right?"

"I guess."

"You *guess*?" Malley frogged me in the arm. "Don't be such a geek."

"Seriously, I'm supposed to take dating advice from *you*?"

"Good point," she said.

"I've gotta ask again. Did Tommy do anything else to you? I mean besides the kissing and the handcuffs."

"God, Richard, why don't you believe me when I say I'm fine?"

"The police are going to ask the same question."

"Then they'll get the same damn answer," Malley snapped, turning her face to the window.

"There's a chance Skink'll kill him, if he hasn't already. You know that, right? He might die himself in the fight, but there's no way Tommy can take him."

"T.C. is strong."

"The old man's stronger. You have no idea."

"Well, good." Malley had flame in her eyes. "Tommy is a monster. Whatever it takes, I don't want him hurting anybody else. Some other girl, she might not be as tough as me."

And that, in the words of Forrest Gump, was all she had to say about *that*.

Southbound on U.S. 331, I went around a battered pickup loaded with bulbous watermelons. The old heap was only doing thirty and the road was clear on both sides, but the passing move freaked Malley out. I couldn't help smiling when she covered her eyes.

"Oh, you think you're so cool," she said.

"It's Driving 101. Be nice and I'll give you a lesson."

"I so can't wait till you get your first ticket!"

The thought had crossed my mind, too. I didn't want to do anything to attract police attention, because Malley and I definitely didn't look like we were on our way to a church picnic—two scruffy teenagers cruising around in a car that didn't belong to us, with thousands of dollars hidden in a shoe box.

Skink's driving mix was playing, the music that had gotten him through Vietnam, he'd said. When a song called "Born to Be Wild" came on, Malley reached to turn it off. Then she changed her mind and turned up the volume. We passed a sign for Eden Gardens State Park, which she thought was funny because my booster-seat book was *East of Eden*.

The rippled shine of Choctawhatchee Bay came into view, and I pulled off at a picnic area on the north side of the causeway. I took some money from the trunk of the car and approached a dock where a heavyset man was hosing down his Pathfinder, a basic open eighteen-foot fishing boat. The engine was a big two-stroke Yamaha.

"Know where I could rent something like this?" I asked.

The man shook his head. "Most places you gotta be twenty-one."

"Seriously?"

"On account of the insurance," he said.

"Oh."

"'Less you do a private deal."

"I've got cash," I said.

The man got thoughtful. I'd never met him before, but there was something familiar about that chubby, sunburned face and oversized balding head.

"You ever run a outboard this size?" he asked.

"All the time," I lied. His engine had five times more horsepower than the one on my little skiff back home. Still, I was pretty sure I could handle it.

"Don't b.s. me, buddy."

"Want me to show you?"

The man licked his dingy teeth and thought some more. "You got any ID?"

I handed over the driver's license that Mr. Tile had given me. The man glanced at my photo, nodded and gave it back.

"I'll pay you two hundred bucks for a four-hour rental," I said. "That's good money."

The man scratched the reddish stubble on his hedgehog chin. "Make it two-fifty—but first I need to see if you know the bow of the boat from the butt."

My cousin got out of the car to find out what was going on.

"Hello, I'm Malley," she said to the man.

"My name's Dime."

The wind shifted and I caught a toxic whiff of B.O. Instantly I made the connection. "You have a brother named Nickel?"

"Sure do," said Dime, "and a sister named Penny."

"Call Nickel, okay? He'll vouch for me."

"He's on his way back from Bonifay, and anyhow he don't carry a phone. And this ain't his boat, it's mine, so git on board. Let's see if you're full a b.s."

Malley watched from a picnic table while I carefully motored Dime around a tongue of flat water that opened into the bay. The Pathfinder's engine needed new spark plugs and the steering felt tight, yet I had no trouble maneuvering to Dime's satisfaction.

One key difference between driving a boat and driving a car is that a boat has no brakes. That means you need to throttle down and coast to your stopping point, or if there's an emergency, slam it straight through Neutral into Reverse, and hang on. All the gears on Dime's engine seemed to be working fine. As the boat gained speed, the rush of fresh air dispersed his foul odor and I could breathe freely again.

I accelerated until the Pathfinder planed off, then I finished the tryout with a smooth 360. Dime took over the controls and steered back to the dock.

"O-right," he said. "Four hours max. But I need a deposit, 'case you two decide to cruise off to Alabama."

"How big a deposit?" Malley asked warily.

"I'd say seven hunnert bucks."

"And I'd say you're rippin' us off."

"Okay, be that way," Dime said. "Good luck findin' you selves a nuthuh boat."

We had more than enough to pay the seven-hundred-dollar deposit, but I wasn't sure that Dime would give it back when we returned. Malley and I had counted what remained in the shoe box: $9,970. It was a huge amount of cash, don't get me wrong, but I thought Skink might need every dollar for medical bills.

I put five fifties for the boat rental in Dime's outstretched hand. "If we're not back by sundown, the car is yours. That's our deposit, okay?"

He snorted louder than the wild boar. "You must think

231

I'm a damn fool," he growled, yet he gave the Malibu a long look over his shoulder.

I tossed him the keys. "My word's solid. You can ask Nickel."

"He's my brother, not my boss."

"Didn't he tell you about the shoe box?"

Dime's brow crinkled warily. "That was yore C-note?"

So now I knew—a hundred bucks was all that Nickel had taken from the buried stash as a fee for ferrying me to the houseboat.

"He earned it," I said to Dime.

"Yeah, well, he shoulda took more."

Malley jerked her chin toward the boat. "How much gas is in the tank?"

"Enough. Y'all ain't goin' upriver, right?"

She eyed him narrowly. "What's the difference where we go?"

"'Cause the river's full a sunk stumps and snags you cain't see," Dime said. "Hit one them suckers and I'll have to sell that car a yours to buy me a new boat."

"Don't worry," I said. "We'll stay out in the bay, where it's safe."

One more lie from the lips of Richard Sloan, but who was counting?

TWENTY-ONE

Malley didn't want to wear a life vest. She said it made her look fat.

"And check out the mildew. Gross!"

"It floats, Mal. That's all that matters."

But the life jackets on Dime's boat were so old and rotted that they tore apart when we tried to put them on. This happened about two miles up the river, after we ran into choppy water during a gusty squall.

The Pathfinder had a center console with a low windshield. To keep my head dry, I fitted on the governor's shower cap, which had stayed crumpled in my back pocket throughout all our escapades.

Malley said, "Okay, now you're creeping me out."

"Don't you believe in mojo?"

"No, but I believe in dweebs, and that's what you look like. Please take off that nasty thing."

"Nope."

On board was the cooler holding our snacks and drinks. I'd also brought the shoe box, to spare Dime from temptation.

Malley pleaded for me to slow down, with good reason. The rain was so heavy that we could barely see ten yards beyond the bow. I eased back on the throttle, scanning the water for obstacles. My cousin unwrapped one of the brick-like subs from the convenience store and gave me half. We each took a bite and made the same sickly face.

"What's your guess, Richard—is this stuff ham or turkey?"

"Vinyl," I said.

But we were hungry, so we forced ourselves to eat. The weather wasn't fierce like the night before. There was no lightning in the dense veil of clouds that settled over the Choctawhatchee, blocking out the sun. We advanced through a strange murky twilight, the hard rain turning to a soupy mist. Every now and then we'd hear the plop of a turtle tumbling from a log, but to our eyes the banks were a haze. At one point my cousin yipped at the sight of a jagged tree limb floating dead ahead, but I'd already spotted it and steered clear.

Eventually we passed another boat, a flat-bottomed skiff drifting downstream. In it was a young couple bobber-fishing for bream and bass. Even in full rain suits the man and woman looked miserable, liked drenched rats. I'm sure Malley and I looked worse. She asked them if they'd seen a white houseboat with a possible hole in the hull, and they said no. The man was using a bait bucket to bail water, which reminded me to check our bilge pump. The wire connections were rusty, like most everything on Dime's boat, yet the bilge was humming like a champ.

"Quick question," said Malley as we motored onward. "Did my parents really put up a ten-thousand-dollar reward, or was that just hype for the billboards?"

"Are you kidding? It was totally legit—ten grand for any tip leading to your safe return. Why does that surprise you?"

"I don't know. It's a lot of money," she said.

"Well, how much do you think you're worth?"

She rolled her eyes. "To them, or me?"

"To everybody who cares about you," I said. "Quit being such a pain in the ass."

She acted startled. "*What* did you just say?"

"You heard me, Mal."

I nudged the throttle forward and kept to the middle of the river—or where I guessed the middle to be. As we rounded a sharp bend, Malley pinched my elbow and shouted. I saw it, too, a bulky object bobbing in the current off the starboard side. The boat was going too fast to stop in time, so I coasted past and circled back.

The thing in the water was a gray hard-shell suitcase, just like the one I'd seen in the cabin of the houseboat.

"Definitely T.C.'s," said my cousin. "See the Mega-Moonwalker sticker?"

The Mega-Moonwalker's Ball was an electronic music festival in Denmark, where Tommy Chalmers claimed to have performed as the star DJ. Malley said anyone could buy the concert decals online for four bucks.

I put the engine in Neutral, reached over the gunwale and hauled the suitcase aboard. "Not very heavy," I remarked.

"Don't ask me. He kept it locked."

Fortunately, Dime had stowed a toolbox on the boat. I took out the screwdriver (rusty, of course) and pried at the latches of the suitcase until they popped open. Inside were the belongings of a professional criminal, not an aspiring musician.

Three license plates from three different counties.

A half-dozen credit cards and debit cards, none belonging to Thomas Chalmers.

Two disposable cell phones.

The blond wig he'd worn when he picked up Malley at the Orlando airport.

A fake mustache that looked like a diseased caterpillar.

A uniform shirt from a pest-control service that had the name "Bradley" stitched on the pocket, a shirt from a cable TV company that had "Chico" on it and a shirt from a septic-tank business that simply said "Supervisor."

And, tucked inside a blue plastic binder, a manila file titled "Malley Spence." The ink was smeared because river water had leaked into the suitcase. My cousin grabbed the binder from my hand and practically clawed it open.

The first page of the file was a printout of a photograph that she'd texted to the man she knew then as Talbo

Chock. There was nothing bad about the picture—Malley in her emerald-green tracksuit, smiling at the camera. Her bony arms were folded and her cinnamon hair was tied in a ponytail, the way she always wore it when she trained.

Without a word, my cousin ripped up the photo, crumpled the shreds and threw them into the water. The rest of the file was notes that Tommy Chalmers had carefully compiled, a profile of his target based on details that she herself had provided.

"Don't tear that up," I said to Malley. "It's evidence."

"Yeah. Evidence of my total stupidity."

"Do *not*—"

But all the papers went flying. They came fluttering down around us, settling in the river as softly as leaves.

I scrambled to find a net to scoop with, but there wasn't one. It didn't matter. Tommy's stalker notes turned to tissue in the currents.

"Let's go," my cousin said. "We've gotta be getting close."

A hundred yards farther we spotted a red bundle—Malley's nylon travel bag. She dragged it dripping over the transom and said, "Okay, Richard, what's the deal?"

"Not sure." I believed I knew what had happened, but I wanted to be certain.

The next item we found was a white fiberglass hatch cover that had snapped off its hinges, followed by the lid of a small toilet seat that I recognized. Ahead of us snaked a bobbing trail of marine debris, which confirmed my fears.

"The houseboat sank," I told my cousin. "All this stuff broke loose when it went down."

She threw up her hands. "So is T.C. dead, or what?"

"Just keep your eyes open."

I steered forward at a crawl.

My backpack and its contents, including *Silent Spring*, must still be at the muddy bottom of the Choctawhatchee. Later, when everything was over, I rode my bike to the Loggerhead Mall and bought another copy of the book, which I finished in four straight nights. I even skipped an evening redfish trip so I could keep reading, which prompted my mother to feel my forehead and take my temperature.

Toward the end of *Silent Spring* is a chapter describing how mosquitoes and certain other insects can become totally resistant to toxic pesticides that had been successfully (and lethally) used against them for years. For example, a Danish scientist reported observing a species of fly frolicking in a bath of DDT, the horribly destructive poison that for a long time was the world's favorite weapon against unwanted bugs. That fly in Denmark had adapted and evolved over rapid generations until DDT was no more harmful to it than a puddle of ginger ale.

How does that happen? The way Rachel Carson explained it, only the toughest and most resistant flies survived all that DDT spraying, and they mated with other tough survivors to produce even tougher ones—superflies that thrived in the face of the same chemical assault that had killed their weaker ancestors.

Survival of the fittest, literally.

When I was done with the book I thought about Skink, who also refused to be exterminated. I wondered to what degree his mother and father and grandparents and great-grandparents were as hardy and resourceful, or if he was simply a supreme freak of nature—one of those rare, random individuals who is blessed with all the strongest traits of his gene pool, and no fatal weaknesses.

Of course he'd ridicule any such description of himself. Yet here is the vision that loomed out of the gray mist in a tailing eddy on the Choctawhatchee River one rainy summer afternoon:

A lone man standing motionless on the water, his ragged reflection encircled in the liquid halo of an eerie bluish-purple sheen.

Not *walking* on the water, Jesus-style, but just standing there, his bare feet (one of them mangled) clearly visible on the surface.

Still impressive, right?

Malley and I might have mistaken him for a holy apparition except for the camo pants and the golf club he wielded as a crutch—an antique nine-iron with a peeling leather grip.

I waved. He waved.

My cousin, who seldom admits to being mystified, said: "Okay, *that* is insane."

"Why, it's the youth of America!" Skink sang out. "Outstanding!"

As we drew closer I noticed a large, unnatural shadow in the depths beneath him, and the shape of it—a pale rectangular platform—became more distinct. The old man wasn't standing on the water; he was standing on the roof of the sunken houseboat.

"Tried to cork that hole in the hull," he muttered. "Too little, too late."

I slipped the engine into Neutral. Deftly the governor hooked the toe of the nine-iron in our bow cleat to hold us in the current.

"You all right?" Malley asked.

"I've been better, butterfly."

A review of his assorted injuries: the deep head gash resulting from his confrontation with Dodge Olney, the pulverized right foot resulting from an eighteen-wheeler running over it; a gory lacework of bruises, scrapes and scabbing punctures resulting from his wrestling match with a mammoth, highly pissed-off alligator.

Now add to this woeful list a through-and-through gunshot wound. The slug had entered beneath his collarbone and exited beneath his left shoulder blade, miraculously missing all vital organs and crucial arteries.

Survival of the fittest, but also the luckiest.

We helped him climb aboard.

"Where's T.C.?" asked Malley.

"Where's the canoe?" was my question.

"Son, I assume you're carrying an anchor. Use it."

With a grunt I heaved out Dime's heavy anchor, which snagged fast on the bottom. The Pathfinder came to an abrupt stop, the bow pointing upstream like a compass needle. I recognized the bluish-purple slick on the surface as oil and gas, leaking up from the houseboat.

Malley's eyes were riveted on the submerged wreck. "Is that where he is?"

"It would have been useful," said Skink, "to know he had another gun."

"Sorry. There was a lot going on."

"You hungry?" I asked him.

"Let's see what you've got."

Malley flipped open the lid of the cooler. The governor grabbed the remaining icky sub, a Snickers bar and two bottles of water, which he chugged. We sat there watching him eat, waiting for him to tell us what had happened. He asked for his ridiculous shower cap, which I was happy to return. He was such a bloody mess that the snail shell covering his eye socket was probably the last detail a stranger would have noticed.

I kept glancing down at the hazy silhouette of the houseboat, half expecting to see the rising corpse of Tommy Chalmers.

"That heron? I asked him why he'd shot at it," the

governor began, "because I believe everyone deserves an opportunity to explain themselves. His answer was unsatisfactory, as was his attitude."

I'm thinking: *Again with the bird?*

"Next we had a discussion about identity theft. To dishonor a fallen soldier like the late Corporal Chock by stealing his name is a loathsome act. Mr. Chalmers didn't exhibit the proper remorse, and I became provoked. I'll take another candy bar."

This time he chose a Milky Way.

"So provoked," he continued with bulging cheeks, "that I made a mistake. I uncuffed him from my wrist."

"Why'd you do that?" my cousin cried.

"Because I intended to launch his sorry ass into orbit, though not before questioning him about the most important topic of all—his treatment of you, Miss Spence. That final conversation grew heated, and he ended it by kicking open an empty battery box and pulling out the aforementioned firearm."

Skink acknowledged the dark O-shaped hole in his chest. It had been plugged with what appeared to be a wad of torn bedsheet. "The shooting was a lapse of vigilance on my part. I was distracted because the boat was sinking, but still, no excuses." He shrugged. "Bottom line, the little maggot shot me."

Malley wasn't the most patient listener. "So, come on, did you kill him or what? Is he down . . . *there?*"

The governor turned his rawhide face to the clouds. A bright green fly landed on his snail-shell eyepiece, and my cousin shooed it away.

He cocked his head. "Hear that?"

"No, sir," I said.

"How about you?" he asked my cousin.

"I don't hear a thing."

"All right." He didn't seem disappointed. "But it's peaceful out here, no?"

"Governor, what happened after Tommy shot you?"

"The bullet knocked me flat. I'm sure he thought I was dead. He jumped in the canoe and went up a creek, literally. The houseboat stayed afloat for another mile or so, then *glug, glug, glug* . . . and here we are."

"The cops'll catch Tommy," I said.

"Really? When?" Malley was upset that he'd slipped away.

"No police," said Skink firmly. "I'm dead, remember? It's a status I prefer to maintain. If I suddenly return from the grave, the authorities will hassle me about certain episodes from the past, some unsolved incidents. Malley, dear, I'm a dreary old fart. My memory's shaky, my temper's short. People say I did this, I did that. Dubious witnesses casting wild accusations, though in a few cases they happen to be true. I've got no appetite to see my name in the news again after all this time. Richard told you my improbable history, correct?"

"He did," said my cousin.

"Then you grasp the dilemma. You're a bright young woman."

"So just disappear. Poof!" I snapped my fingers. "We'll cover for you, make up a great story."

Skink noticed Tommy's suitcase propped upright against the transom. "Did you two peek inside? I'm guessing it wasn't Bibles."

Malley spoke up. "What if there's a trial? Would it be, like, totally my word against his?" She strained to hide that she was dreading it.

"No jury will believe a word that jerk says," I asserted. Then to the governor: "We'll take you straight to the car, then you just drive off into the sunset, right? I brought the shoe box, so you'll have plenty of money. Let the police go find Tommy."

"Maybe they can, maybe they can't," he said. "But here's a fact: *I* can find him. Right now, Richard, with this excellent vessel you've provided."

"Listen, he's sick as a dog. He won't get far," I argued. "The cops'll catch him by this time tomorrow, and you'll be long gone."

"And if he gets away? Hitches a ride, hops a train, flees the state? Think of the harm he might cause to somebody else's cousin." Skink helped himself to a Coke.

Malley wore an expression that crushed my heart. Whatever Tommy Chalmers had done to her, the damage was written on her face. She'd made it through that ordeal the same way Skink had always prevailed, through sheer unstoppable will.

"I do *not* want him to get away," she said.

"He won't." The governor and I said it at the same time.

"Hey, it's not like I'm scared to testify," said Malley. "I'll do whatever it takes."

But there were more tears than raindrops on her cheeks. The last time I'd seen her cry was at my father's funeral.

Facing T.C. in a courtroom would be rough, him sitting there all clean-cut in a new coat and necktie, pretending to be some sort of model citizen. I understood that Malley needed to see him caught on the river, to be there in person, not just go home and trust the police to find him. She needed the final word, a final *something*.

I did, too. I admit it.

"You're not going after Tommy alone, no way," I told the governor. "We're coming with you."

"Definitely. Done deal." Malley's tone was sharp. "And don't even think about throwing us overboard again, okay? That sucked."

Skink was in full predator mode, too preoccupied to argue. He burped volcanically and jammed the empty Coke can in the cooler.

"YOLO," he said.

Then he reached for the rope and hauled up the anchor as if it were weightless.

TWENTY-TWO

I let him take the wheel. Like I had a choice.

When he rammed the throttle down, the bow porpoised once and then we were skimming full-speed up-river, weaving around stumps and logs. Malley and I clung to the rail of the boat—a radical thrill ride with no seat belts.

We made it to the creek in five minutes. The governor cut the engine and signaled for us not to speak. Besides the thump of my own heart, the only sound I heard was the boat's wake sloshing against the bank.

Quickly Malley got restless. She pointed to the narrow entrance of the creek and mouthed the words, "Let's go!"

Skink ignored her and closed his good eye. He looked like a grizzled old iguana. The rain had quit, and amber stalks of sunlight punctured the clouds.

A gunshot went off, the echo pinging through the trees. Skink turned sharply toward the sound. From the same direction came a second shot. Moments later a gangly, wide-winged bird came veering from a gap in the creek, then rose and crossed the river, flapping furiously.

Another heron, only this one was as white as cotton.

The governor restarted the engine. "Here we go, boys and girls."

Slowly he steered the boat up the creek, which was lined with palmettos and bright wild azaleas. My cousin sat beside me on a cushion in front of the console. She edged closer, whispering, "T.C.'s got three bullets left."

I'd already done the grim math. Even though I'm not into guns, I know most revolvers are six-shooters. Tommy had used one round on Skink and two just now. That left a slug each for me, Malley and the old man.

The only advice that came to mind: "Be ready to duck."

"Really, Richard?"

It's impossible to explain why we weren't completely paralyzed with terror as we closed in on this desperate, trigger-happy sicko. Having Skink there calmed us, though Malley and I were also aware that he was freakishly fearless, abnormally immune to the threat of a loaded weapon.

Soon we came upon the canoe, which had been dragged out of the water. On the bank lay Skink's spinning rod, which Tommy probably had found too challenging to operate with only one good hand.

The governor slotted the Pathfinder through a patch of reeds, beached the bow and stork-stepped to the bank, steadying himself with the nine-iron. Sternly he told us to stay where we were.

"Get real," said my cousin.

Skink looked to me for a vote of support, but I said, "We'll be right behind you. Let's go."

The landing was mucky and roped with vines. Talk about pig paradise—everywhere you turned the dirt had been trenched, trampled or pawed. Palmettos and pine saplings lay in mauled clumps, their roots chewed to pulp.

Maybe that's what Tommy was shooting at, I thought. *Another wild boar.*

I was the only one in bare feet, the price being a gnarly green thorn in my right heel. Malley yanked it out with her fingers. Ahead, Skink stooped like an old-time gold prospector as he followed the kidnapper's meandering tracks.

None of us spoke a word.

This is a part I didn't learn about until later. Some of the details I've filled in on my own.

With four hours to kill and some real money in his pocket, Dime had decided to take the Malibu for a joyride, undoubtedly thinking: What could possibly go wrong?

He was dating a woman near Mossy Head but she wasn't home, so he backtracked to DeFuniak Springs and wheeled into a roadside bar for a drink (possibly two). He was cruising back toward Choctawhatchee Bay when a plain dark sedan appeared in his rearview.

Dime thought nothing of it until he saw the flashing

blue light on the sedan's dashboard. Nervously he steered the Chevy onto the shoulder, braked to a reasonably smooth stop and scrambled to invent a believable story. Nothing clever sprung into his head, not one decent idea. His palms were damp on the steering wheel.

The officer wore street clothes—a striped golf shirt, beige pants and brown loafers. He was a muscular African American man with close-cropped white hair, and he looked considerably older than most of the uniformed cops Dime had dealt with. Yet a cop he most certainly was, a semiautomatic on one hip and a badge from the Florida Highway Patrol on his belt.

Dime couldn't see a name on the badge. He was trying not to get too close because he had liquor breath in the middle of the afternoon, a condition generally frowned upon by law enforcement. The trooper didn't ask for his driver's license or demand to see the registration and insurance papers for the Malibu. Instead the conversation went something like this:

"Sir, where did you get this car?"

"It's my uncle's."

"Wrong answer," said the trooper. "Try again."

"Okay, it belongs to a friend a mine."

"Strike two." The trooper opened the car door and told Dime to get out.

A light rain was falling, but from the thickening clouds Dime knew heavier stuff was on the way. He stood slack-armed and dejected while the big cop patted him down, the cop old enough to be his grandpappy except he was the wrong color.

Dime didn't want to get charged with auto theft or driving under the influence, and he most definitely didn't want to go to jail. He'd been there before. Afterwards he had promised his pappy (and himself) that he'd never give the law any reason to lock him up again, even for one night.

"Okay, here's the God's honest truth," he said to the trooper, "but it's gonna sound sort a crazy. First off, I ain't on drugs."

"That's good to know."

"Every word I'm 'bout to tell ya is true as the gospel."

"Let's hope," the trooper said.

Dime spun through the story about renting his boat to a couple of kids, a boy and a girl who seemed way too young to be tooling around the county in a Chevrolet. About how they paid him with cold cash and left the car as a security deposit—a perfectly good vehicle!—keys and all.

"That's more like it," said the trooper.

"You believe me?" Dime was so relieved that he could have hugged the man.

"Tell me where they went."

"For a ride on the bay."

"You know for a fact?"

"Well, yeah. I tole 'em to keep outta that river."

"Do you have another boat?" the trooper asked.

"Not my personal self," said Dime, feeling a thousand percent better about the situation. "But I know where I can git one."

We get so hooked on being connected 24/7 to our friends, our playlists, our Tweets and Instagrams, whatever. The battery in our smartphone dies and it's like somebody shut off the oxygen to our brain. *Where's my charger? I can't find my stupid charger! Mom, drop everything and take me to Radio Shack!*

That's me. I'm definitely attached to my phone. Malley always gets crazy stressed whenever her parents confiscate hers, which happens on a regular basis due to her acting like a smartass brat. Without her cell she's unbearable, mean as a moccasin. And when her computer freezes, she turns pure psycho. One time she threw it against a wall and cracked the screen. I'm not quite that bad, but my mood turns foul when my laptop crashes.

It's amazing how soon you forget your electronic pacifiers when they're at the bottom of a river, how easy it is to stop fixating on all the texts, messages and posts you might be missing. Not once did Malley and I gripe about being isolated from our precious social networks. Pursuing a desperate criminal through the wilderness drastically rearranges your priorities.

Skink had survived war and a multitude of other

perilous adventures. My cousin had survived a kidnapping, and I'd survived the hunt to track her down.

If luck was an ingredient, how much did we have left?

"Don't look up," Skink said.

"How come?" Malley asked.

On the ground we saw where Tommy Chalmers's footprints abruptly stopped, as if he'd been plucked off the planet by some aliens in a spaceship.

"He's in the tree," the governor reported in a murmur.

"Which tree?"

"The one we're under. Keep your voices low, act confused and do *not* look up."

The black dirt around the trunk was pitted by jumbo pig tracks. A wild boar had chased Tommy way, way up a pine.

"There's fresh blood on the bark," said Skink.

"So what do we do?" my cousin asked. Then, purposely louder: "Gee, which way do you think he went?"

We were both trying so hard not to look up that we were staring like morons at our own tracks in the muck. Skink said we should continue walking, circle back through the woods and wait for Tommy to climb down.

It sounded like a decent plan, except Tommy didn't cooperate. We'd taken only a few steps before a hoarse voice crooned from above:

"Why, there she is! My sweet, beautiful bride!"

Skink spat a curse word. More than one, actually.

"Can we look up now?" Malley asked archly.

Tommy sat on a branch, his legs dangling, the gun held in his left hand. His right hand, the catfish hand, had swollen so grotesquely that it might as well have been inflated by a bicycle pump. The fingers didn't resemble real fingers anymore—more like scalded purple sausages. In fact, the whole arm was bloated all the way to the shoulder socket, as if he was wearing one of those padded tubes used for training police dogs how to maul crooks.

"Hi there, sweetie," he called down to Malley. "You been missin' me? Now, tell the truth."

"You need a doctor, T.C. You look like poop on a Popsicle."

My cousin, smooth as ever.

"Come on down from there," she said.

"Ha, not with *him* around." Tommy waggled the pistol barrel at Skink. "Or him, neither."

I admit I flinched when he pointed the weapon in my direction.

The governor said, "We're not armed, son."

"You got a spear!"

"Naw, it's just a golf club."

"Shut up, dude, it's a spear! I already shot you dead once, so are you some kind a zombie or what?"

"I'm just an old man who wants to talk."

"No, a swamp zombie with a spear is what you are!"

Tommy was nearly delirious from the infection, though

you couldn't blame him for not wanting to tangle again with Skink. He wasn't the least bit afraid of me; I was just a ninety-five-pound nuisance.

Malley said, "Then I'll tell them to leave. It'll just be you and me, T.C."

Under his breath the governor said to my cousin, "Bad idea, butterfly."

"Okay, but I got three bullets left," Tommy hollered down, "say they get any bright ideas to come back for you. I shot at some dumb hog that got on my case, I'm not afraid to shoot a zombie."

I wondered if Tommy believed in Bigfoots, too.

"You heard the young lady," Skink said to me. "Let's go."

Of course we would be coming back for Malley. We'd be coming back for Tommy, too.

Side by side Skink and I began to walk. He said, "This will happen fast, so be sharp. Your job is getting your cousin out of the way. Do whatever's necessary, Richard, but leave me a clear path to Mr. Chalmers. *Comprende?*"

The governor was smiling, naturally. As calm and casual as if he were strolling to the post office.

After disappearing from Tommy's line of sight, we doubled back in silence, approaching the tree from a different direction. Skink pointed to a fluffy wax myrtle shrub, and we crouched behind it, spying.

Tommy had begun an unsteady descent from the pine, raining broken twigs and scabs of bark. He looked like a drunken scarecrow. The seat of his jeans had been ripped open, exposing a pimply crescent of gouged buttock where the angry boar had implanted a tusk. That explained the blood smears on the tree trunk.

When he finally reached solid ground, Tommy gave a feeble pump with his gun hand, yelling, "Oh yeah! Killed it!"

The governor told me to get ready.

Tommy held out his unbloated arm, beckoning my cousin for a hug.

"You poor baby," she said sweetly.

Then she stepped forward and slugged him in the belly. It sounded like a sledgehammer hitting a sack of wet rice. He crumpled, goggle-eyed and wheezing, but he didn't let go of the gun.

Skink was already on the move, crutching his nine-iron through the marsh bottom at a surprisingly zippy pace. I dashed past, grabbed Malley by the waist and pulled her off to the side. The governor was kneeling on Tommy's neck, prying the pistol from his fingers.

My cousin broke free and ran back to kick and punch at her kidnapper. She was calling him names, screaming questions.

What made you do it?

How did you pick me?

Why'd you lie?

What's wrong with you?

T.C. didn't say a thing. He appeared half-conscious, loose-jawed and limp as a dirty rag.

Once again I dragged Malley away. Skink let go of Tommy and stood up, barking like a deranged pit bull, and I mean *barking*. It was more startling than one of his loud dreams, because he was wide awake.

After dumping the remaining bullets from the gun, he beat it against a maple tree until the cylinder broke apart and the barrel snapped. Then he began chanting in some unrecognizable language while performing a cripple-step jig that was even weirder than Malley's pig-scaring dance. All the time he kept spinning that nine-iron like a drum major twirling a baton.

Malley and I sat wordlessly watching the governor's bizarre fit, which we hoped would freak Tommy into a petrified state of surrender.

Finally Skink switched back to English. "I got blisters on my fingers!" he brayed before keeling facedown.

We figured he was just taking a rest; acting wacko had to be exhausting.

Unfortunately, he wasn't acting. The fit he'd pitched came from the same dark place as his nightmares, and the timing couldn't have been worse. But maybe a self-induced collapse was his subconscious way of stopping himself from killing Tommy Chalmers with his bare hands.

As we struggled to flip Skink over, we noticed he didn't seem to be breathing. He felt like deadweight, and dead is how he appeared, his chin whiskers frothed with white spittle.

The next thing I remember is Malley cradling his head

while I pounded on his bruised chest trying to remember CPR from the class that Mom made me take after Dad died. My cousin and I both noticed Tommy struggle to his knees and start crawling off, but the lifeless governor held our undivided and frantic attention.

I pushed down so hard on his rib cage that the wadding blew out of the bullet wound beneath his collarbone, followed by a spurt of dark blood.

I pushed down so hard that the snail shell got ejected from his eye socket.

I pushed down so hard that his hips bucked in a violent spasm that flung me like a cowboy from a rodeo bull.

The crusty old lunatic sat up coughing. "You ruined," he said between hacks, "a perfectly good trance."

Malley retrieved his snail shell. Tartly she sniped, "Gee, sorry for trying to save your life. I don't know what Richard and I were thinking."

My hair was full of wet dirt and leaves. "Dude, we thought you were dying," I said to Skink. "You looked really, *really* bad. Much worse than . . ."

"Usual?" He gave a razor-edged chuckle. "I'm just curious. Did either of you happen to notice where Mr. Chalmers went?"

TWENTY-THREE

During the commotion Tommy had crabbed back to the canoe and shouldered it down the bank. Now he was paddling along the creek, an awkward and noisy effort with one arm swollen to the size of a Yule log.

"I hate you! I HATE YOU!" Malley shrieked from the shore.

For a moment I thought she might dive in to give chase. As sick and woozy as he was, Tommy still knew which way to go: Toward the river.

With a lopsided leer he called back to my cousin: "You'll see me again one day, honey, don't you worry! I know where you live. I know which school you go to. I know *everything* I need to know about you!"

Malley whirled toward Skink. "Why'd you break the gun? That was so . . . so . . . STUPID!"

She grabbed the golf club from his hand and flung it at the canoe. The nine-iron pinwheeled harmlessly over Tommy's head and splashed into the creek.

The governor got into the Pathfinder and turned the

key. The engine shuddered but didn't start. Again and again he tried, until only a dull clicking noise came from the ignition switch—another sign of Dime's loose approach to boat maintenance.

"Hell," said Skink, and a whole lot more.

From the canoe Tommy continued taunting my cousin. "We'll get married just like I said, don't you worry! On a beach somewheres far away, just me and my dream bride. . . ."

He was paddling faster than I thought possible for a man in his wrecked condition, faster than any of us could swim.

Skink clambered from the boat and snatched his fishing rod off the ground. The same bass lure was still tied on the line—a skirted spinner with two sets of treble hooks, meaning six total barbs. The hooks weren't large, but they were plenty sharp enough to pierce human flesh.

He began casting at Tommy while he gimped along the bank, crashing through bushes and skidding across tree roots, trying to keep pace with the moving canoe. Although the creek wasn't wide, you couldn't safely wade in it because the bottom was basically quicksand.

The governor's aim was off the mark again and again. The lure sailed left of Tommy, then right. Short, long, longer, then short again. Tommy wasn't ducking out of the way—in fact, he was completely clueless, huddled in the bow carving feverishly toward freedom. His good arm did the stroking while he used the bloated one to steady the paddle, those gross sausage fingertips hooked over the handle.

"Here, let me give it a shot," I said to Skink.

He handed me the rod—no argument, no lectures. I couldn't believe it.

On my very first cast I snagged the back of Tommy's shirt and jerked firmly to set the hooks. He yelped, dropped the paddle and started swatting at himself. I'm sure he thought he'd been stung by a big-ass bumblebee.

I tried to keep the pressure tight but the drag mechanism buzzed, line peeling off the spool as the current carried the canoe away. Skink's light spinning tackle wasn't designed to crank in a hundred and seventy pounds of anything—fish, man, or beast—though I knew some extraordinary catches had been made by skilled anglers on flimsy tackle. I pictured myself heroically yanking Tommy into the river and hauling him kicking and hollering to the shore, where we'd tie him up with vines and hold him for the police.

But of course that isn't what happened.

Tommy did end up in the water, though not because I had a burst of superhuman strength. He flipped the canoe all by himself while flailing around, trying to dislodge the unseen killer bee.

This occurred outside the mouth of the creek, a full one hundred yards from where I stood holding the bent fishing rod, Skink on one side of me and Malley on the other. We could see the glinting hull of the capsized canoe clocking down the rain-swollen Choctawhatchee.

T.C. wasn't moving quite as swiftly, because he was still attached to me. The spinner's treble hooks held fast.

"Don't let him get away!" Malley shouted. "Reel him in, Richard! Reel fast!"

But he was too heavy, and now the muscle of the river began carrying him along. He didn't panic. We could see him lifting his head taking deep breaths. There was no frantic spluttering, no desperate howls for help. Tommy was just riding the current, paddling with his good arm.

"Stop him!"

"I can't, Mal!"

Helplessly I watched the spool empty as Tommy was drawn farther and farther away. If I tightened the drag knob, the line would snap for sure. There was nothing to do except hang on and hope he swung into the calmness of an eddy.

The governor said, "It's over, son. Break him off." His lone eye was fixed intently downstream.

"Over? Seriously?" My cousin stomped up and down. "Are you like totally lame? That monster's getting away! He is getting *away*!"

"Not likely," said Skink.

An instant later, Tommy Chalmers went under in a fierce boiling swirl, and my line went slack.

I reeled in. The lure was gone, still hooked to Tommy. I put down the fishing rod and sat on a stump.

Skink said, "'Nature teaches beasts to know their friends.' That's a quote from Billy Bob Shakespeare himself, though he was not personally familiar with crocodilians. Now, I'm gonna take a stroll and clear my brain."

He grabbed my shoulder and said, "You keep close to her."

"I will, don't worry."

"Remember our rule, son. There was only one, for God's sake."

"I remember."

"Do whatever I say, whenever I say it. And now I'm telling you to stay right here, both of you, no matter what. I won't be far."

"Okay."

At the boat he stooped to retrieve his shoe box, which he tucked under one arm. Before clomping away he said, "You're one of the good ones, Richard."

Whatever that meant.

Malley didn't see him go because she couldn't look away from the rolling river. Her gaze was locked on the spot where Tommy had disappeared.

"What just happened?" she said.

"Gator."

"Did you see it?"

"Skink saw it."

"But did *you*?" she demanded. "'Cause I didn't see anything, Richard."

Gently I turned her by the shoulders and showed it

to her—the dull black brute pushing a wake, its ridged back as wide as train track, its long tail slicing a leisurely S in the water. The alligator was already halfway across the Choctawhatchee, but there was no mistaking what was jackknifed in its open jaws.

The green of the T-shirt, the dark blue of the jeans.

"Really" was all my cousin said. Then she sat down, shaking.

We stayed quiet at first, each of us trying to deal with what we'd just seen. Malley finally asked where Skink went, and I repeated what he'd told me—to stay where we were, he wasn't far away. She thought we should go find him, but I said no, not this time.

The rims of the clouds were pink and rose, sunset colors. A good breeze brought a faint smell of salt from the Gulf. There was a soft shuffling in the woods behind us, and Malley and I turned expectantly. Nobody was there, although later she insisted she'd heard a hushed voice telling us to look up.

I'm not sure what I heard, but for whatever reason we both raised our eyes.

Poised high in a moss-draped cypress was the Lord God Bird, one bright eye slanted down toward us. The woodpecker was a full-grown male, regally tall and more vividly colored than the drawing we'd used for my science project. Its blue-black breast feathers gleamed like coal, and a snowy stripe sloped down its neck and fanned at the tail. His long, flat-tipped bill truly looked like raw ivory.

And the crest on the crown of his head was a shade of crimson brighter than blood.

"I told you so," she whispered. "Told you I saw one."

"Amazing." It was the only word that sprung into my mind, and it seemed too small for the occasion.

The great woodpecker made a squeak like a dog's chew toy when you step on it, or maybe the rusty hinge of a screen door. Three times the bird repeated the call, but no other ivorybill replied.

Everyone's memory works differently, so I can't honestly say how we long we sat watching that supposedly extinct creature—or more accurately, how long it sat watching us. The whole time we remained motionless, as still as moths on a leaf. Maybe it was five minutes, maybe it was thirty seconds. My cousin isn't certain, either.

"Surreal" was her description of the encounter, a better word than mine.

After the woodpecker flew away, our eyes remained fixed for a while on the top of that tree. We knew the bird probably wasn't coming back, just as we knew the governor probably wasn't coming back, but that didn't stop us from hoping.

Malley and I weren't the ones who spooked the ivorybill. It took off because a boat came around the bend of the river.

The gar man's barge, grinding and chugging. We smelled it almost as soon we saw it.

At the helm was Nickel wearing his goofy NASCAR

shades. Beside him stood Dime, a frowning, slightly shorter, less scruffy version of his brother.

A third figure sat sideways on the gunwale. He wore a casual short-sleeve shirt, his thick arms folded across his chest. I could see the white cap of hair, and the gun in the holster on his belt.

I waved my arms and shouted, "Mr. Tile! Over here!"

The trooper nudged Nickel, who adjusted their course until the reeking vessel was headed straight for us.

"Well," said my cousin, "I guess we're officially rescued."

TWENTY-FOUR

I didn't want Nickel and Dime to hear me, so I whispered to Mr. Tile that Skink was in the woods.

"Who?" he said.

I guess that was their arrangement. Whenever the governor decided to disappear, Mr. Tile would let him go, no questions. He understood that the old man needed more personal space than the average human. About a thousand times more, I'd say.

Skink left because he'd heard Nickel's boat coming long before we did. He seemed to hear and see everything before we did.

As the gar barge motored away from the creek, Malley and I scanned the shoreline hoping for one more glimpse—a wave, a wink, anything. I don't know if the governor was watching us, but we wanted to believe he was.

"Skink got shot," I told Mr. Tile.

"Who?" He wrapped an arm around my shoulders, pulled me closer and said, under his breath, "That friend of ours is a hard man to kill. If he's on the move, he's gonna be all right."

I used Mr. Tile's phone to call Mom, who was super-relieved to hear my voice. I mumbled something about the taxi breaking down again and Mr. Tile driving by just in time, a totally lame story that I'm sure didn't fool her for a moment. She spared me the lawyer treatment, though—no cross-examination. She was too happy that I was coming home. Afterwards Malley spoke with Aunt Sandy and Uncle Dan, whom she described as "insanely overjoyed."

Mr. Tile got rooms for all of us at a motel in Panama City, and the next morning we left for Loggerhead Beach. It turns out he and my mother had been talking, like, three times a day. The only reason she hadn't freaked out and called for an Amber Alert was that he kept telling her I was all right, even when he wasn't so sure.

Mom didn't know about the intense situation on the river, and neither did Mr. Tile. When he found the gray Malibu by the Road 20 bridge, he figured the governor and I had gone into the woods tracking the fake Talbo Chock and my cousin. Mr. Tile went to hire a helicopter, but then the weather turned lousy. When he returned alone to the bridge, the Malibu was gone.

He caught up with it later that afternoon, Dime squirming in the driver's seat. Afterwards they went straight to Nickel's place and launched the gar boat. It had taken them less than half an hour to find us on the Choctawhatchee.

The car ride back to Loggerhead Beach took all day. When I jokingly offered to split the driving time, Mr. Tile laughed and made me give back the counterfeit license. The Malibu was already on a flatbed heading for an auto auction in Atlanta. Mr. Tile explained that Skink never used the same vehicle twice, and he preferred projects that required no driving on his part.

"Was all that cash in the shoe box his?" I asked.

"Years ago he came into some money, which he told me to give to charity. Without telling him, I set aside a few bucks for his future well-being, just in case." Mr. Tile winked. "Good thing I did."

I rode in the backseat because Malley wanted to sit up front so she could dominate the musical selections. The sedan didn't have satellite radio but she found a tolerable FM station that was Bieber-free. Mr. Tile even let her turn on the dashboard blue light once, when no other cars were around.

He asked us lots of questions about Tommy Chalmers, but he didn't press Malley for every ugly detail of the kidnapping. He was a total gentleman about it.

On the subject of Skink, he had little more to say except that they were old friends who understood each other very well. We told the trooper (who was retired, as I thought) how the governor had collapsed unconscious after pitching a whacked-out fit; how we thought he was actually dying but then he popped up like nothing was wrong and told us it was just a trance.

"Who knows," said Mr. Tile.

"Aren't you worried about him?" Malley asked.

"Every minute of every day."

"You told that reporter he was dead," I said. "I saw it on the Internet."

"That was his idea. What do you two plan to tell the police about your colorful travel companion?"

I looked sideways at Malley. She shook her head.

The trooper said, "Do whatever you think is right. He'll understand."

"He who? I don't know who you're talking about," I said. "Some stranger gave me a ride up to the Panhandle. Dude wouldn't even give his name!"

Mr. Tile chuckled. "That works."

"The problem is my mom. She knows who 'he' really is."

"Your mother's extremely grateful that you and your cousin are safe and sound. I'm guessing she's not interested in causing any grief for the governor."

Mr. Tile's cell went off, a plain default ringtone. The conversation lasted several minutes. He did more listening than talking. After he hung up, I asked if it was Skink on the other end. He said no, it was the sheriff of Walton County, another old buddy.

The body of Malley's kidnapper had been discovered by a fisherman. It was wedged under a floating tangle of branches where the gator had hidden it for leftovers.

However, the dead man was not Thomas Chalmers. That name had been stolen from a shrimper in Dulac, Lousiana, who'd been killed by a lightning strike two summers earlier.

The fingerprints of the corpse in the Choctawhatchee River belonged to a person named Terwin Crossley, age twenty-six. Born in Hattiesburg, Mississippi, Crossley was last known to reside in Valparaiso, Florida, where he'd stated his occupation as roofer. His rap sheet listed convictions for armed burglary, forgery and aggravated stalking.

The initials T.C. were the only true information about himself that he'd given to my cousin.

"I am such a stupid idiot," she said, her voice raw with despair.

"No, you're just young," Mr. Tile told her, "and he was a bad, bad guy."

There was more news from the sheriff, he said. "At 3:37 a.m., a UPS truck driver called 911 about a suspicious person in the road—"

"Wait," I cut in. "You're talking about today?"

"Yes, early this morning," the trooper said. "The truck driver reported a person kneeling by a roadkill in Ebro, a couple miles west of the Choctawhatchee bridge. The driver said the dead animal was either a coyote or a stray dog that had gotten hit by a car. The man in question had a pocketknife in one hand and the driver thought he looked mentally unbalanced."

"Shocker," said Malley.

"He was wearing camo trousers and a woman's shower cap. The UPS guy honked so he'd get out of the way."

"What happened?" I asked.

"The man dropped his pants and mooned the truck." Malley cheered. "Major style points!"

"He was gone by the time the deputies got there," Mr. Tile reported. "So was the coyote."

"Oh well," I said. "It's better than leeches."

The day after we got home, Detective Trujillo interviewed me for a couple hours. He never once asked if the person who gave me a ride upstate was Clinton Tyree, former governor of Florida, so technically I never had to lie about meeting the man. Some old stranger drove me to the Panhandle is what I said, which was close enough to the truth.

The detective didn't ask me about exotic woodpeckers, either, and why would he?

Back when I didn't believe the ivorybill still existed, Skink had warned me that if word of a sighting ever leaked out, the river basin would be overrun by tour boats, swamp buggies and roadside souvenir shops, all sorts of greedheads trying to make a buck off the bird. He'd said the one he saw might be the last of its kind on the entire planet, or maybe the first of a hardy new generation, but either way it deserved peace and solitude. He might as well have been talking about himself.

I put the ivorybill in this story because it's key to what happened, the main clue that led me to Malley. I also don't believe anybody's going to see that particular bird again until it chooses to be seen. Same goes for Skink.

My cousin spent like five hours talking with Detective Trujillo and a female officer. After that, the case was officially closed and the "Help Us Find Malley" billboards were taken down. The police department put out a press release saying she was home safe and asking the media to respect her family's privacy. The press release also said that the suspect in Malley's abduction had accidentally drowned before the authorities could apprehend him. The gory details were left out.

That gray suitcase full of evidence, which we'd brought back for Detective Trujillo, ended up in a police warehouse somewhere. There was nobody to investigate, nobody to arrest. Terwin Crossley had acted alone, and died alone.

In fairness to alligators, they don't often kill human beings. It happens at most once or twice a year, which sounds like a lot until you consider that Florida has more than one million wild gators and eighteen million people. Statistically, bumblebees are more deadly.

The first thing my cousin did when she got home was rinse the black dye from her hair. A doctor checked her out, and she's going to be fine. The handcuff marks on her wrists have already faded away. Once a week she goes to see a counselor—"head shrinker," in Malley's words—and honestly I think it's helping her, even though she says the lady smells like petunias and vinegar.

Sometimes Malley and I talk about what took place on the river that afternoon. We saw a man die, and we've both had bad dreams about that. T.C. was a rotten guy but it was still a gruesome thing to see.

If I hadn't snagged his shirt with the fishing lure, he probably wouldn't have toppled into the water, and the alligator wouldn't have grabbed him. On the other hand, he wouldn't have been out there in the first place, trying to paddle away, if he hadn't done anything wrong.

I've got no idea what kind of childhood Terwin Crossley had, whether his parents were kind and loving, or cold and cruel. Maybe he was one of those kids who never had a chance to become a decent person, or maybe he was born a creep.

Either way, I'm not brokenhearted over what happened to him, not after what he did to Malley, not after the twisted threats he made from the canoe. As far as I'm concerned, the gator that ate T.C. deserves a medal from Crime Stoppers. Maybe I'll go straight to hell for saying that, but it's the truth. I can't speak for my cousin, because she's never put that particular thought into words.

We'll never know if the animal that took Terwin Crossley was the same one that had swum off with the canoe two days earlier. After the kidnapper's body was recovered, state wildlife officers set out baited hooks in the area. That's standard procedure after a fatal alligator attack, and they almost always nab the culprit.

Not this time, though. They didn't catch anything, not even a dumb garfish.

Mostly what Malley and I wonder about is whether Skink somehow knew what would happen to T.C., even before the gator appeared—whether it's possible for a person to be so powerfully connected to nature that he develops an almost mystical kind of intuition. The governor's reaction to that shocking scene was so mild and matter-of-fact that you couldn't help but wonder if he was expecting something like that all along.

Malley's not a hundred percent convinced he did, and neither am I.

I do believe, though, that some things aren't meant to be understood. And I also believe in karma.

I've never told my mother that Skink taught me how to drive. My plan is to surprise her when I get my learner's permit.

One weekend we went to Saint Augustine to see Kyle and Robbie, who were there for a surfing contest. On the way up, Mom semi-casually mentioned something you might call a cool coincidence, and also ironic: Her own mother, my late Grandma Cynthia, had handed out campaign buttons and bumper stickers for Clinton Tyree all those years ago when he ran for governor. Weird but true.

That night after dinner my brothers got me alone and quizzed me about the Malley adventure. They said I had "balls of steel" for going to find her all by myself. It took every ounce of self-restraint not to tell them about Skink, who in my mind was the true hero of the rescue.

Not to mention one of the coolest old farts ever.

Just about everything he told me was true. The Rousseau novel he quoted from is called *Émile*. The Shakespeare line he tossed at us came from a play called *Corialanus*. "Sporange" is a real word ("a cellular structure where spores are produced"), and it really does rhyme with orange.

The governor was also right about Linda Ronstadt— she's got an awesome voice. I downloaded her *Heart Like a Wheel* album after my mother bought me a new smartphone to replace the one at the bottom of the river. I offered to pay her back, but she said no.

Which worked out okay, because I needed the money for something else. I'd gone back to work for that carwashing service—and I mean, every day—so I had exactly two hundred bucks in my fist when I walked into the surf shop in Saint Augustine.

The owner, Kenny, my dad's friend, was behind the counter. After I counted out the cash, he said, "Thanks, dude," and put it in the drawer of the register.

"Don't you want to know what it's for?" I asked.

"The skateboard you took last year." Kenny was smiling. "Look up," he said.

A bubble-eye video camera was mounted on the ceiling above the counter. I counted three more in the store.

"So you knew all this time it was me who stole it?"

"You didn't steal it, Richard. You just forgot to pay. I knew you'd be back one of these days."

"You did? How?"

"Because you're Randy's son, and that's what he would have done."

"No, he would never have taken it in the first place."

"Maybe he would, if he'd lost his dad when he was young and needed something special to keep the memory close," said Kenny. "You tried that board yet?"

"No, sir."

"Well, you should. It would make him happy."

After I got back home, I pulled the Birdhouse from my hiding spot in the box springs beneath my mattress. I didn't want Mom to get sad if she saw it, so I waited until she left for the office before I put on my helmet and rode the board down A1A.

Damn, it's fast.

Obviously, Malley didn't have to go away to the Twigg Academy. After everything that's happened, I think Uncle Dan and Aunt Sandy would love for her to stay at home until she's, like, thirty-five. They were seriously shaken up. Malley promised to cut back on the daily drama, which she has, so far. Her parents call or text her all the time, which is understandable, though it annoys Malley.

School started last week, and she's a major celebrity because of the kidnapping. The attention makes her really uncomfortable, which is epically *not* like my cousin. She even shut down her Facebook page and got off Twitter. In the halls kids sometimes stop her to ask about T.C.—who he was, how he chose her—and she tells them just enough of the bad stuff to make sure the same thing never happens to them.

A few days ago she broke the seventeen-minute mark for the 5,000-meter run. It would have been a state cross-country record for a girl her age, except it didn't happen at a track meet. Malley had been running by herself with her stopwatch early in the morning at the high school. She does this all the time. She says nobody bothers her because nobody can catch her.

What she doesn't know is that she's never really alone when she runs. One of us is always hanging around near the track, out of sight, just to make sure there are no fake Talbos on the scene. Some mornings I'm the designated lookout. Other days it's Uncle Dan, Aunt Sandy or Mom. Even Trent helps out. We've got our hiding spots.

T.C. is no threat to Malley anymore, but all of us who care about her are still extra protective. Maybe that will change someday, but I'm not so sure.

Speaking of Trent, he finally sold two houses, one of

them a sweet oceanfront estate. To celebrate he bought my mother a jade necklace, got himself a new set of golf clubs and gave me a supernice fly rod.

Then he took us to dinner at his favorite steakhouse and, okay, I couldn't resist asking if he'd ever heard the legend of the Florida swamp zombie.

"What the heck's a swamp zombie?" he said, all intrigued.

"It's like a Bigfoot, only smarter and gnarlier. I actually saw one in action. He had buzzard beaks hanging from his face."

My mother knew who I was talking about. She gave me a don't-make-fun-of-your-stepfather look.

"Never heard a that one," said Trent, hitching an eyebrow. "Are you bustin' my niblets, champ?"

"Yeah, I am. There's no such thing as a swamp zombie."

The next night I had my first so-called date with Beth. We went to a Will Farrell movie and she laughed almost as loud as me, which was a good sign. Next weekend we're going fishing on my skiff near the inlet. Beth officially broke up with Taylor, so everything's cool in that department.

Except now Taylor keeps texting Malley begging her to go out. She's told him to get lost in, like, thirteen different languages, literally. Malley's got an app that translates her snarky insults into Spanish, French, German, Greek, I forget all the others.

My cousin can be brutal.

Mr. Tile left a voice message saying I should go online and read an article that appeared in the *Pensacola News Journal* just a few days after we left Walton County. Check out the headline:

ANONYMOUS DONOR HONORS FALLEN MARINE

The story said an unknown person had opened a scholarship fund at Northwest Florida State College in the name of the late Earl Talbo Chock, a young Marine corporal killed by a roadside bomb in Afghanistan.

What made the donation curious was the odd amount—$9,720—and the fact that it was all cash, delivered by the postal service in a plain shoe box along with a short handwritten note of instruction.

According to the newspaper, Talbo Chock's mother and father were eager for the mysterious benefactor to come forward so they could properly thank him or her for the generous memorial. They said a tall homeless man had recently been observed at their son's gravesite, standing ramrod straight, saluting the plain white cross. When a cemetery worker approached him, the stranger made a "crude gesture" and limped away.

Talbo Chock's parents wondered if that was the same person who'd sent the shoe box full of cash to the college, and they asked for the public's help in identifying him.

I tried calling back Mr. Tile at least half a dozen times, but his phone went straight to voice mail. He had nothing more to tell me, I guess. He just wanted us to know Skink was all right. I printed out the article and gave it to Malley when we went on one of our turtle walks.

The three-quarter moon looked like a ripe peach coming up over the ocean. I'll never forget the color of the sky because that was the first night my cousin and I found a mother turtle on a nest.

We'd walked less than a mile before we spotted fresh flipper tracks leading from the edge of the surf to the dune line. There, an enormous barnacle-backed loggerhead had dug out a pit as wide as her shell. When I shined the light down the hole, we could see her eggs dropping softly.

The turtle didn't snap at us or try to crawl away. She just blinked her big moist eyes and took short raspy breaths, a tired old momma with a job to do.

She'd been there before, and her female hatchlings that survived to adulthood would return to the very same beach, the very same time of the summer, to lay their own eggs. It is a ritual that's only been going on for about a hundred million years. Incredible but true—loggerheads, greens and hawksbills were swimming the seas back when T. rex was roaming the forests.

Malley and I took photos of the mother turtle, but we didn't post them on Instagram. Instead we called a state wildlife hotline and gave the location of the mound. Tomorrow there would be bright stakes hammered down, and a warning sign. With any luck, Dodge Olney was still locked up in jail.

We didn't want to attract a crowd that might disturb the momma loggerhead, so we kept walking. Every so often we'd find a scattering of crispy egg fragments where other nestlings had hatched, a stampede of little hockey pucks toward the surf. Some of them had made it, and others had been gobbled by gulls or raccoons. That's the natural food chain, but Malley and I still always root for the baby turtles.

At each marked nest I paused to aim my flashlight at the dig marks inside the bright pink ribbons. A few times I dropped to my knees because I thought I'd spotted something out of place, but I hadn't.

During these odd stops of mine Malley never got impatient or even slightly sarcastic. It was something I'd been doing on our beach walks ever since we'd returned from the Choctawhatchee, something I'll probably be doing the rest of life.

Looking for a soda straw sticking out of the sand.